"A wild, funny, poetic fever dream that will change the way you think about America. Durkee is a true original—a wise and wildly talented writer who knows something profound about that special strain of American darkness that comes out of blended paucity, materialism, and addiction—but also, in the joy and honesty and wit of the prose, he offers a way out. I loved this book and felt jangled and inspired and changed by it."

—**GEORGE SAUNDERS**, author of *Lincoln in the Bardo*

"This book's a blast! A super-long shift in the life of a north Mississippi taxi driver makes for hilarious moments as well as lyrical ones. Durkee's Mississippi is entirely his own as he parades a line of passengers that are as colorful, sad, and strange as any in literature. A terrific novel by a terrific writer!"

—**TOM FRANKLIN**, author of *Crooked Letter, Crooked Letter*

"*The Last Taxi Driver* is unpredictable, emotionally moving, and laugh-out-loud funny. Lee Durkee writes with honesty and deep insight. This book is filled with compassion. I loved it. The best book I've read in years."

—**CHRIS OFFUTT**, author of *Country Dark*

"It may be the worst day of Lou Bishoff's life, but *The Last Taxi Driver* is a frenetic, voyeuristic delight. A Mississippi Buddhist doing his best to be kind, Lou ferries around meth heads and rehab escapees, drives overgrown frat boys to and from drug dens, and wonders at what point he stops being a cab driver and starts being an accomplice. Timely and compulsively readable, Durkee's long-awaited second novel makes me regret how much I've missed by being a (reasonably) sober and compliant passenger."

—**MARY MILLER**, author of *Biloxi*

*N*

"A stone cold masterpiece. Haven't felt this way since reading *Jesus' Son* and *Bringing Out the Dead* for the first time. Raw, revelatory, honest, full of kindness and anger and sadness and compassion."

**—WILLIAM BOYLE**, author of *City of Margins*

"For devotees of the offbeat and grit lit writers like Larry Brown and Mary Miller. Follow the air freshener rocking back and forth, taking you under its spell, as Durkee takes you for a ride."

**—THE A.V. CLUB**

"One of the best novels in recent memory. . . . A wild and hilarious ride."

**—*WASHINGTON EXAMINER***

"Much of what makes Lee Durkee's novel so delightful and surprising is his ability to dig beneath the surface of this funny, well-told odyssey, which channels a Shakespearean tragedy. This twenty-year follow up to his debut novel, *Rides of the Midway*, was worth the wait."

**—CHICAGO REVIEW OF BOOKS**

"A gonzo ride full of dark humor, philosophical insights, and shrewd observations about the plight of luckless people in the United States."

**—SHELF AWARENESS**

"*The Last Taxi Driver* is a road novel . . . rooted firmly in our America. The novel almost makes other fiction in that Southern tradition seem frivolous by comparison."

**—RAZORCAKE**

"The working-class realism of Charles Bukowski with the counter-cultural flamboyance of Hunter S. Thompson . . . Yet somehow, the author creates such a vivid likeness of life that readers can't help but feel uplifted. There's beauty in the beastliness. Don't miss this one."

—*LUCKBOX MAGAZINE*

"*The Last Taxi Driver* is a *Canterbury Tales* for our time . . . Decentralized, atomized, and alternately tranquilized and jacked up on cheap beer and meth, this is the world of Beckett, Godard, Robbe-Grillet."

—**FULL STOP**

"In Lou, Durkee has created a fascinatingly complex character . . . Durkee tackles race and poverty, violence of many varieties, loss and longing, and the power of the imagination. Lou's excruciating day will make readers cringe, and the recounting of his traumas is more than unsettling. This is a dark, feverish, and weird tale that remains compelling throughout."

—**BOOKREPORTER**

"The funniest writer you've never heard of, but that may change. His 2001 debut, *Rides of the Midway*, is a 1970s coming-of-age master-piece . . . Now, nearly twenty years later, at last we have Durkee's second book, his own reboot, and wow is it worth the wait . . . a future Tom Waits vehicle if there ever was one."

—**JOHN FREEMAN**, Lit Hub Executive Editor

Published by Tin House, Portland, Oregon

Distributed by W. W. Norton and Company


Library of Congress Cataloging-in-Publication Data

Names: Durkee, Lee, author.
Title: The last taxi driver / Lee Durkee.
Description: Portland, Oregon : Tin House Books, [2020]
Identifiers: LCCN 2019031489 | ISBN 9781947793392 (hardcover) | ISBN
    9781947793484 (ebook)
Classification: LCC PS3554.U6865 L37 2020 | DDC 813/.54--dc23
LC record available at https://lccn.loc.gov/2019031489

First US Paperback Edition 2021
ISBN 9781951142681 (paperback)

Printed in the USA
Interior design by Diane Chonette
www.tinhouse.com

# The Last TAXI DRIVER

## LEE DURKEE

 TIN HOUSE / Portland, Oregon

*To the saints of the service industries.*

*And in memory of Ron Shapiro.*

A man takes a job, ya know? And that job—I mean, like that—that becomes what he is. You know, like—you do a thing and that's what you are. Like I've been a cabbie for seventeen years. Ten years at night. I still don't own my own cab. You know why? 'Cause I don't want to. That must be what I want. To be on the night shift driving somebody else's cab. You understand? I mean, you become—you get a job, you become the job. One guy lives in Brooklyn. One guy lives in Sutton Place. You got a lawyer. Another guy's a doctor. Another guy dies. Another guy gets well. People are born. I envy you your youth. Go on, get laid, get drunk. Do anything. You got no choice, anyway. I mean, we're all fucked. More or less, ya know?

—**WIZARD**, *Taxi Driver*

It's just a ride.

—BILL HICKS

# OPPOSITE EARL

They never tell you what they were in for, only that they just got out. This one's a handsome white dude—mid-thirties, a few missing teeth, a few prison tats—who's in a fantastic mood. He's carrying a twelve-pack of Bud Light when he slides into the back of my Town Car and tells me he's just been released from Parchman and then gives me the name of some street in the Bethune Woods Project, says it's an old girlfriend's house.

"Man, is she gonna be surprised to see me," he adds.

We're at the Mobile station near West Gentry Loop waiting to pull into traffic.

"Maybe you should call her first?" I suggest to the rearview.

"Man, I don't even know her number been so long. She's probably married-divorced twice."

We hit the four-lane and head east toward the largest of the five projects I didn't know existed before I started driving a cab. These projects are arranged like black moons around a white planet, and it's my job to ferry kitchen workers into the square or wherever it is they work, a twenty-dollar bookend on a job that pays them maybe nine bucks an hour.

It's late spring midafternoon but already feels like summer as I drive under the Fordice Bridge past campus. As I do this I'm wondering if Uber will steal all my rides from the projects. I've never used an Uber and don't understand how that works, but my hope is that when they come into town next month—it's not just a rumor anymore—Uber will shun the projects the same way all the other cab companies in town do.

Bethune Woods is one of our nicer projects. It has a suburban façade filled with the evilest speed bumps in town fronting the grim rows of public housing apartments.

"Damn," my fare says as the Lincoln bottoms out on a speed bump.

"You get used to it," I tell him.

"Is it yours?"

"Nah, company car. I get to keep it at my house. I mean, as long as I put in my seventy a week, I do."

"Seventy hours? Man, that sounds kinda dangerous."

I laugh and tell him, "I know guys drive ninety."

Our destination turns out to be a beater house. Somebody has stolen the garage door, and a plastic wave of kid junk is cresting into the driveway. The lawn is that bright green ryegrass with brown jigsaw pieces where somebody sprayed ant poison. The one catalpa tree is either blighted or a late bloomer. No cars. All the lights off.

"Man, can you wait here a minute? I'm just gonna look-see inside."

Leaving his beers on the floorboard, he rings the bell and waits, combs his hair back with his fingers, then knocks and waits some more. Finally, after glancing back at me, he wanders into the garage, pokes around in there, and then opens the side door and disappears into the house.

I sit there thinking, *well, I didn't see that coming,* and once again I find myself wondering what makes an accomplice an accomplice. At what moment do you stop being a taxi driver and start being a getaway driver? But I don't leave, not yet. For one thing, I haven't been paid. Also I happen to like the guy. He looks like a discarded version of my friend Earl, who hustles golf for fun. This guy is like Earl's prison twin—Rich Earl, Poor Earl—the Earl who owns nothing and has lost a few teeth in Parchman. Same year, same model: opposite fates.

Opposite Earl gets back into the cab lugging a pilfered six-pack of High Life bottles to add to his floorboard collection.

"Man, she ain't even here. You mind taking me out to 243? I know this other girl. I can't remember the street but I can point you there."

"Pays the same," I say, my way of letting him know I'm not taking him there for free. I should tell him it's two bucks a mile outside city limits, plus two bucks each additional stop, but instead I start telling him about my friend Earl.

"He drinks Bud Light, too. Y'all look so much alike it's crazy. When I first saw you standing there I was sure you were him."

"All he does is play golf?"

"Yeah, I guess. He wins all the local tournaments—they call them *scrambles*—and he doesn't even practice. I don't think he even likes golf."

"That how he got rich, hustling golf?"

"No. He was born that way."

"We really look that much alike?"

"Twins," I say, and then think, well, except for that neck tat depicting the great state of Mississippi.

"So where's this guy live at?"

I hesitate and then tell him, "Out on 40."

"What'd you say his name was?"

"Earl. Earl Jones."

I am a bad liar. It always sounds like I'm asking a question.

"Huh. You think I could fool his wife?"

I don't comment on that. Earl's wife is my friend Kyla, who does not fool easily. We turn onto 243 near the Soul Food Stop and wind our way into some suburb near the county middle school. It's a much nicer house this time but has a ramped driveway that causes the Lincoln to bottom out again. Like I said, you get used to it. He knocks on the front door, does his hair again, then removes a key from under the doormat and goes inside. This time, he comes out with a corked bottle of red wine and an orange.

"Maggie ain't home, either," he tells me, and a moment later I hear the cork pop. "Man, I ain't had wine in fuck forever. Ain't the only thing I ain't had."

"Please don't peel that orange back there," I say.

"No sir," he replies, in what I assume to be the voice he used in prison to talk to guards.

I've started driving us toward the house of this third girl he knows when we are passed on the road by a robin's-egg-blue '57 Chevy convertible.

"Wow," I say.

I never cared about cars before driving a cab. Now I like them better than I like most people.

"That's her!" he yells. "That's Maggie's Chevy—catch her!"

I gun the twenty-year-old broke-dick Lincoln. It takes about ten minutes and five gallons to catch up, and right as we do the Chevy turns into a gas station and it becomes clear the platinum blonde behind the wheel is accompanied by some guy with the largest bald head I've ever seen. His meaty arm draped over the passenger door is covered in those Japanese gangster tattoos, like sleeves that end at the wrist.

"Fuck. Man, let's get outta here."

Opposite Earl stays glum for a few miles but then rallies and still wants to go to this other girl's house. I tell him I won't take him there unless he promises not to steal anything. In total he has four ex-girlfriends. Either that or he's just scouting houses to ransack later. None of the women are home. Finally he makes me take him back to the first house, the one in the project, and I charge him twenty bucks—the freedom-is-sweet special—and leave him sitting in a lawn chair in front of the doorless garage drinking wine and looking happy. That's what she'll see when she pulls into the driveway that evening with her kids.

As I coast away, he grins and lifts his wine bottle. I start to honk but then remember my horn doesn't work. Then I start to wave before remembering the tinted glass. Then I wave anyway.

# STINK BOMBS

Pardon my French, as my fares like to say, but you'd be freaking amazed by the smells that enter my taxicab. The numerous funks, farts, fumes, burps, breaths, bombs, and auras—odors that defy description—my least favorite among them being the putrid, seaweedy stench of frat-boy spit cups. Under the driver's seat of my Town Car I keep a fat bottle of Ozium and a thin bottle of Aloha Febreze. I have a pine-scented Bigfoot air freshener dangling amiably from my rearview below a Shakespeare-mint freshener modeled on the NPG's Chandos portrait. Above Shakespeare hovers a Lazarian-style flying saucer with wintergreen-spiced Zeta Reticulans spying out its portholes. Also scattered around my cab is a pawnshop display of those baubled air fresheners advertised in checkout aisles to last a week in your vehicle, which translates into a day in the life of a Mississippi All Saints Taxi cabdriver.

I'm parked at the town square facing the Oasis Diner and thinking about Opposite Earl, about how maybe we all have a worthless or

wealthy doppelgänger, and maybe that's how the world evens itself out
and makes life on earth fair. Is it possible that Rich Earl and Poor Earl
are somehow the same being who has been divided into two or two
hundred people? I'm always trying to come up with theories that make
life fair, though of course it isn't. If there's one thing this job driving
twelve- to fifteen-hour shifts seven days a week has taught me, it's that
life ain't fair.

Pretty soon I catch myself talking out loud again—something
that's been happening a lot lately, even with fares in the car—so I shut
my mouth and shrug at the car camera. *Whoever told you life was fair,
kid?* That question comes to me via my dead father's gruff-drunk
voice. My father loved asking me that. Every time I complained about
anything, I got hit with that question. And now, forty years later,
parked in a cab I don't own waiting for my next dispatch, it seems to
me as if men are driven crazy by this notion of fairness. Maybe for
women it's obvious early on that life isn't fair, but men cling to the
idea of fairness. We murder and go to prison and hang ourselves over
it. Little boys especially worship fairness.

It's 5:00 PM now and I've only got one hour of unfairness left on
my shift. Even this late in the day, the long black hood of the Town
Car is simmering like asphalt. Although it might appear I've started
reading a paperback, in truth I'm zoning out and letting the letters
crawl around the page when a text message bings in from Horace, my
supervisor, telling me to fetch a fellow driver—this guy Zeke—and
take him to the garage we use out on Ross Barnett Road.

Only All Saints uses text messages to dispatch. Every other company in town—and there's about ten of us, all ragtag—still uses the
traditional radio, but Stella, a devout Catholic who started All Saints
thirty years ago after receiving a Fátima-like vision from God, became

paranoid that other companies were stealing our rides, so now we use messages, which means we're constantly text-weaving in traffic.

Before fetching Zeke, I swing by my place to use the head. My house is one of those bungalows that were once servant quarters. A bunch of frat boys live in the big house in front of me. They've got Confederate flags in their windows, and they're always parking in my slot or blocking the driveway with the giant SUVs daddy bought them for making straight Cs in some seg-ed prep school.

Much to my nonsurprise I find my girlfriend Miko asleep on the bed—that's pretty much all she does these days. She suffers from depression, a soul-sucking condition that renders me equally lifeless whenever I'm around her. She's a poet, or used to be, and a good one, so I suppose she's entitled to a certain amount of ennui, but it's getting absurd. Sometimes I suspect it's her lethargy that allows her to remain so beautiful, seemingly as young as ever, while I by contrast age in time-lapse fashion. I desperately need to get Miko out of my house and out of my life—her suicidal thoughts permeate my dreams at night—but she's broke and helpless and I'm all she's got in the world.

I tiptoe past the bed into the bathroom. The toilet, which needs cleaning, is situated next to a window also in need of cleaning. While standing there peeing, I automatically start searching for the three-legged doe that haunts my backyard ravine. Her name is Maya and she's about six months old and there's nothing graceful to her gait, but she owns a great dignity and I am her champion. In the mornings she stares at my windows until I come outside and throw my breakfast strawberries at her. I've counted as many as fourteen deer in my backyard and almost that many groundhogs. When the grass is tall I get red foxes. My cat Bandit stalks them all or pretends to.

Today I spot Maya and her dangling stump half hidden in kudzu. It's hard to feel sorry for yourself while staring at a three-legged deer. My guess is she got hit by a car, but it's possible a dog got after her or some drunk frat boy shot her leg off for fun. Or maybe she was born that way. As I stare at the hobbled doe—her Bambi spots are gone now—I try to perceive her without attraction or aversion, like the Buddha advised, to somehow absorb her dignity without fixating on the ugliness of her stump or the direness of her fate. I've started rereading Miko's books about Buddhism lately in an attempt to stop myself from flipping everybody off. So far it's not helping. If anything, I'm getting worse.

On the way outside, I stop to study Miko and try to decide if she's faking sleep, but how can you tell? Her back is to me and she's naked and her long black hair is spilled across her thin shoulders onto the mattress. Back in my cab I head toward Choctaw Drive to fetch Zeke. I'm still thinking about life being fair. I'm thinking the only way earth could be considered fair is if we agreed to come down here on our own volition, like it's a video game we stupidly decided to play. Either that or earth's some kind of reform school and we did something terrible to get sent here.

Zeke, the driver I'm picking up, is about forty years old and sometimes takes his daughter out with him at night. His daughter is ten and must help considerably with tips. And his daughter is about the only reason you'd tip Zeke, who looks like a redheaded version of the Unabomber and wears bright superhero tee shirts that coalesce over his beer belly like poured oil.

I pull into Choctaw Ridge Apartments to take him to the garage. The driveway is lined with overflowing dumpsters that turkey buzzards are orbiting high above. The moment Zeke enters my cab his stench stun-guns me. It's like being electrocuted by cat piss. Tears start running down my cheeks. After a minute of suffering I manage to clear my throat, swallow painfully, and ask Zeke what got fixed on his van. Getting anything repaired by Stella requires a prolonged lobbying process, one or two near-death experiences, and a few screamed threats to quit.

"Brakes," Zeke grunts.

"Brakes? No way. I've been begging brakes for months, man, and I been driving for Stella a lot longer than you have. Listen to these things."

I hit the pedal, which goes to the floor and shudders obligingly.

"Front and back," I say proudly.

"Tough tit, man. Hey, you really from Vermont?"

The area code on my cell is still 802, which inspires a lot of redneck repartee.

"Nah, I just raised a kid up there. Eighteen years, man. Eighteen fucking winters. It damn near killed me. I'm from south Mississippi originally. Hattiesburg."

"You're from Tough City?"

"Yeah, but I never knew they called it that till I moved here."

"You sure don't talk like you're from there. You been crying or something?"

"No," I reply, trying to shelter him from the truth about his body odor. "It's just, you know, allergies."

Zeke keeps staring at me in a peculiar way. As he does this, his eyes twinkle with what seems at first to be a Kris Kringle merriment. It's the beard and John Lennon glasses that create this illusion, but it isn't merriment, I suddenly realize, it's menace. Or maybe it's the twinkle of insanity, of secret diatribes and homespun bombs. Why the hell did this freak get brakes instead of me? All the day-shift guys think Stella favors the night shift. I am resisting the urge to phone her up right now and give her a piece of my mind. In my imagination I quit grandiloquently every day—I am the Cicero of quitting—but in real life I don't quit because I desperately need the job. I have two grand to my name plus a shabby condo in Vermont nobody wants to buy. I'm mid-fifties and worried sick about the future. Retirement? As far as I can tell this Town Car is my retirement.

"Enjoy your brakes," I say petulantly as we shudder-squeal to a stop at Jim Warren Automotive. The last time the Town Car got an oil change here somebody stole the jack out of the trunk, and I still haven't talked Stella into getting me a new one.

No jack, no horn, no brakes. It's not fair.

Zeke opens the door and then points to my gaggle of air fresheners and asks, "That Bigfoot?"

"Yeah. It's pine-scented."

"I saw him once," he says and gets out and slams the door without even telling me about it.

"Yeah?—did y'all like murder cats together?" I shout once he's out of earshot.

Then I reach under the seat and go Rooster Cogburn on the Lincoln: the Ozium in one hand, Febreze in the other. His poor daughter, I keep thinking. And the world seems to me at that moment to be filled with great herds of three-legged deer staggering through endless woods.

# HOSPITAL RUNS

Stella likes to say that day-shift cabbies are the fabric that holds the town together, that we're as important as any utility, and sometimes I think she's right. While the night crew hauls around scrums of Adderall-vomiting co-eds and makes twice the jack we do, the day shift takes citizens to work, mostly black people in the service industry. We cart the halt and lame to Kroger and lug their groceries up flights of stairs for dollar tips. We spring upstanding citizens from bail bondsmen offices and squirrel them across town to the impoundment lot behind the Toyota dealership. We deliver rich people cigarettes and serve as care managers for the elderly—I've done everything from helping old people pee to taking out their garbage to chasing after their escaped pets. We are the poor man's ambulance, and we are also, sad to say, the poor man's priest, our cab the confessional in which people litmus-test their wildest fears and prejudices.

All Saints, being one of the oldest cab companies in town, has a contract with the local hospital so that when somebody dirt poor—and this is the most dire state in America, Third World in parts—when somebody destitute in north Mississippi is being released from the hospital, All Saints will deliver them to wherever they abide—usually the Delta—and our fee is added to their bill and eventually paid for, I assume, by taxpayers. The only good thing about these deathbed runs is that Stella charges the hospital mileage both ways. A nurse I've got a crush on once called me out on that, and I laughed and assured her I earn every penny I make off hospital runs. She thought that over and said, "Yeah, I bet you do. We give y'all the dregs, huh?"

The *dregs*. Not a kind word but not untrue. Taxis traffic in the desperate. People at the end of their ropes eventually stagger into cabs.

On my very first hospital run—almost two years ago, right after I'd gotten fired from the university—I picked up this fifty-something white guy who had told his dentist over the phone that he was going to shoot himself in the head if he didn't get a stronger pain pill. The dentist reported this to the police, who sent over a cruiser. The two policemen explained to the guy that he could go to the hospital with them or they would call an ambulance, which would be expensive, and they would place him into the ambulance whether he wanted to go or not. Through his toothache the guy told the cops he'd only been kidding about shooting himself and wasn't going to any damn hospital. The ambulance arrived and the cops made him get inside it, and he spent all that day in the psychiatry wing getting interrogated about suicide.

By the time I picked him up it was dark, a dismal, drizzling evening in early winter.

"Seems like a man oughta have the right to kill himself anyway," he fumed from the back seat.

I agreed. I said, "Yeah, that's kinda the most basic human right there is, huh?—the dying middle finger."

I didn't tell him about my father or my grandfather or how suicide runs in my family. Instead I asked if the hospital had given him anything for the pain. Sometimes fares will tip you pills.

"Hell no. Fucking Motrin was all they give me. Hey, speaking a which, you mind swinging by a liquor store and maybe fronting me some whiskey? I'll pay you back soon as we get to my house."

I thought that over.

"Sorry, man. No can do."

"Yeah. I don't blame you that."

We stayed quiet until we pulled into his driveway, when he said, "I wonder if my TV dinner's still safe to eat."

Like a lot of men do, he leaned forward to shake my hand before he got out. And that night, while falling asleep to dream about phantom tips, phantom cheapskates, phantom speed traps, and phantom deer smashing through my windshield, I thought about that guy reheating his TV dinner and smelling the plastic compartments—the gooey Salisbury, the shriveled peas, the wet-cement potatoes—trying to decide if it was indeed safe to eat.

By the time I get Zeke's smell out of the cab, my shift is all but over. I park at the square and stare at the digital clock in spite of knowing that's bad luck. Sure enough, one minute before six the Bluetooth rings inside my ear.

"Good news," Stella says. "I got you a double."

"A double?" I reply, not bothering to hide my irritation. "But—"

"But nothing, mister. You're up next so don't give me a hard time. You're driving everybody crazy with your complaining. You should thank me. It's a hospital run. Twice the mileage, half the gas, baby."

Instead of thanking her I give her a cold dose of silence. There are few things crueler than the end-of-the-shift hospital run, and Stella damn well knows it. All the cabbies hate hospital runs because Stella won't pay us until the hospital pays her, which can take months, and, unless you're vigilant, Stella will either forget to pay you or will underpay you and then wait to see if you notice.

I want to tell her it's not fair, but instead I ask, "ER or out front?"

"Front, dear," she replies in the maternal voice she uses once she's gotten her way.

I almost hang up on her but don't.

"Zeke told me he got brakes," I hear myself say, which scares me. I'm afraid all my frustrations might pour out in one obscene stream-of-consciousness jag.

"That's because the fool got in another wreck."

"Oh. Is that what I got to do, Stella, get killed to get brakes?"

"Let's talk brakes tomorrow. Right now you need to go to the hospital before I get angry. I'm having a good day so don't fuck it up."

With that, she hangs up on me.

I flip her off. Unless I tell you otherwise I am always flipping somebody off.

Five minutes later I pull into the hospital and grab my receipt book and walk inside. Chloe, the nurse I like, only works the ER side, but I can't help looking around for her—I've got it bad for Chloe. I estimate the mileage, fill out the forms, get the supervisor's signature, and photograph the receipts so I can keep track of how much Stella is ripping me off. That done, I sulk back to the cab and wait for my two fares to arrive.

While waiting, I put on Beethoven—I tend to start and end the day with his piano sonatas—and then sneak a hit on my Snoop

Dogg–endorsed G Pen and blow the white smoke directly at the car camera ceaselessly staring at me and imagine that smoke emerging into Stella's living room, where she sits watching my every move like a soap opera called *As the Wheel Turns*. I'm still staring down the camera when the two orderlies wheel out my fares side by side. One fare is black, the other white, and it's hard to decide which one will keel over in my back seat first. Trust me, they don't release these patients because they're cured, they release them because nobody is footing the bills. Generally speaking, it's my job to whisk them to their deaths. In that sense I am like Charon, the shaggy boatman who ferries shades across the River Styx.

> There Charon stands, who rules the dreary coast—
> A sordid god: down from his hairy chin
> A length of beard descends, uncombed, unclean;
> His eyes, like hollow furnaces on fire;
> A girdle, foul with grease, binds his obscene attire.

As soon as my passengers are belted in, I turn around to study them. I'm trying to make sure I'll be able to get them out of my car and carry them up whatever stairs might be required. In this instance, I could probably lift both of them at the same time, one under each wing. These guys are as desiccated as old mushrooms you could kick into dust. Neither of them has luggage. The black guy, who looks a hundred if a day, is still wearing his hospital gown and hardly nods when I say hello to him. He'll probably die first, I decide. The long-faced white guy, by contrast, is eager to yak and quickly informs me that he's a farmer and has survived seven surgeries in the last five years. "That must be some kinda record," he shouts in the manner of the half deaf. He looks to be mid-eighties with a face made of rubber and he's grinning like a hellcat and lifting up his shirt to show me all the scars I don't want to see. Meanwhile the older guy beside him keeps staring around the cab like he's watching the path of a wasp. What's he looking at? Ghosts, I decide.

I'm taking the black guy to Clarksdale, but first I'm dropping off the farmer somewhere on Highway 9. When I ask the farmer his address, he says there isn't one, but he can point me there.

"My trailer's off Terza Road. You know where that is?"

"I know where everything is," I tell him.

Music-wise I select Sonata no.13 in E flat, a piece that suffers from a sad and beautiful schizophrenia, all its moods and movements wildly different yet blended together perfectly—almost like Beethoven let himself get possessed by different demons one after another while composing it. Turning up the volume so I won't have to keep talking to the farmer, I drive down the highway twelve miles to a county road flanked by young cotton. Eventually the farmer points me toward a fallow field, where we follow a tractor path through high grass—grass taller than the cab—and after ten minutes of squeaks and groans we arrive at a rusted trailer. I undo the padlock with his key and then go back to the cab and fetch him out, get an arm under him, and limp him up the cinder-block steps and push the door open upon a dark room containing one metal chair. The room reeks of Vicks VapoRub. A bunch of grasshoppers are flying around the wedge of sunlight I've let inside. After sitting him in the chair, I look around and ask if he has anybody taking care of him. A grasshopper lands on his cheek and I brush it away. Another one lands on my neck and I slap at it. "How you gonna eat, mister?" I ask. I know he'll be stuck in that chair, and in the horrible heat, until somebody else arrives. How can he go to the bathroom? Is there a bathroom? All I can make out in the dark is a stunted countertop with a propane camp stove and a P-38 can opener.

"Who's taking care of you?" I shout into his deafness.

He shouts back that his brother lives nearby. Two more grasshoppers have landed in his white hair—one is navigating the pink river of his part line. I nod, glance around again, then shrug and shake his hand and tell him, okay, good luck, and leave him sitting there in that oven of darkness as I drive away through the high grass in my creaking Lincoln with the fleur-de-lis magnets stuck on the sides.

It isn't until I emerge from the field that I think to phone the hospital. When I do, they promise to call his brother and double-check the situation. And that's that. The old deaf guy with the seven scars is gone.

With dusk closing in, I hurry to Clarksdale, home of the Delta Blues Museum and Morgan Freeman, but it's the Bloods and Crips and Vice Lords on my mind as I speed through Batesville, where the landscape flattens out and the color seems to seep out of everything, like opposite Oz. Usually I love driving in the Delta. It feels like I've crossed an ocean and landed on a new continent with new rules. Many of these rules, it turns out, have been made by drug gangs. The Delta is famous for its lack of law enforcement. Cops are considered an anomaly.

Twilight finds my Town Car turning onto King Street. It occurs to me, not for the first time, that the Lincoln fits into the projects far better than I do. My kitty, a metal cashbox with my log sheet clamped on top, is in the front seat with about 160 bucks inside. I find the address and stop. As I'm lifting the old man out of the car, his hospital gown comes untied and suddenly he's standing there naked beneath the stuttering streetlight. Meanwhile a dozen or so black kids holding 40's start walking toward us. This is not good. Not good at all. I am trying to retrieve his gown from the street when some unknown woman arrives to rescue me by saying, "I got him. Get outta here, mister," and that quick I jump behind the wheel, hit the gas, and immediately veer to avoid colliding into two teenagers who have stepped in front of my grille. This keeps happening, more young men stepping out of the darkness to block my escape. I slalom between them and take the first left at a squeal.

The Delta projects are tiny houses, mostly brick, with pit bulls or hunting dogs chained to the fenders of sunken sedans. "Holy shit," I keep repeating as my heartbeat slows and the houses keep clicking by. But, at the same time, I wouldn't trade it. Seriously, it beats walking home from campus with a cache of semi-racist essays to grade. In some ways I'm glad I got fired from the university, though I'm certainly not proud of how I got fired. I'd rather die in the Delta, I guess, than spend my life explaining the uses of a direct object to some piss-stained frat boy.

During the drive home I start wondering if those kids back there were actually gang members. Probably not, I decide. But that's another thing that happens with this job: you accumulate idiot prejudices left behind in the back seat among the antidepressants and hair extensions. You listen to enough racist yabber and pretty soon find yourself believing that any black kid holding a 40 is a Vice Lord. You swear off your prejudices but they keep accumulating. You vow away traffic tantrums yet the car camera keeps recording them. And most every day you learn there is a limit to your kindness.

I'm that rare beast, a Mississippi Buddhist, and I used to think I was a good Buddhist, or a decent one, before taking this job. Now I know better. Now I know I am the worst Buddhist in the world. And one of the reasons I know I am a horrible Buddhist is because of the ghost of a young girl I did not show enough kindness to. In certain slants of light, particularly around dusk, I can glimpse her in my rearview, all Gothed-out and mascara-smeared, weeping inconsolably.

This girl who will haunt my cab forever was about twenty and had just lost everything moments before being shoved into my cab by sheriff's deputies. I'd answered a dispatch five miles north of town and pulled up to a house with four prowlers parked out front, their flashing blues almost invisible in the Mississippi sun. Eventually four deputies came over with this young white girl who was weepy and snotty and carrying a black baby who was weepy and snotty and screaming. The troopers pushed her into my back seat and ordered me to get out of there or they were going to arrest her too. It was like they hated her for having a black baby but not quite enough to throw the two of them in jail. I hesitated, glanced at the girl in the rearview for the first time, not knowing she'd be there forever, then I rolled down the one automatic window that still worked and told the nearest deputy we needed a car seat for the baby.

He gave me the hard eye and said, "Drive. Away. Now."

The girl cried out, "They won't let me take nothin'—not even diapers."

I said, "C'mon, sir, we gotta have a car seat—that's the law."

Perhaps realizing this was being recorded on my camera, the deputies conferred, then a younger officer was sent back to the house, where God knows how many men were sitting handcuffed on the floor of their meth lab. He returned holding a battered car seat so decrepit I half expected a rat to crawl out of it as I buckled the thing into the back and then drove off with the baby screaming and one of the prowlers tailing us for five miles just to be a dick.

The baby obviously needed a new diaper, but it felt rude to reach for the Ozium. We drove past Gentry's Creekside Project, which had been condemned a few weeks earlier, to a small house at the end of a red clay road. The girl, who owed me about twenty bucks by then, handed me six dollars in balled-up snotty bills, and then starts counting change out of a grayish ziplock baggie. Finally she handed me the whole snotty bag. I gave her the change back but kept the bills. And that's what I've felt wretched about ever since. What the hell was I thinking? Here she'd just lost everything, and I didn't even give her a free ride? What kind of human being could be that cheap?

Nobody was at the house when I drove off. I didn't ask if there was some other place I could take her. No, instead of helping that kid out, I pocketed her last bills and left her standing on a porch in front of an empty house holding a hungry baby with a stinky diaper. I could have bought her some diapers, man. It wouldn't have killed me. I could have bought them groceries.

But it had been such a long week, with so little sleep, that I didn't even realize what a jerk I'd been until later that week when I told the story about the meth bust to my friend Vance, who interrupted me at the moment in the story when the woman was handing me the snotty bills. Putting himself in my shoes, Vance said, "Keep it lady, sheesh." Like he knew, being my friend, that I'd never have considered taking those bills. But I had taken them. And I was so ashamed of this fact that I let Vance believe I hadn't taken that baby-food money, but I had, I'd palmed those snotty bills, and now, confronted with my friend's faith in me, I saw myself in a revealing light, a quick vision of a soul resembling a meth-head mug shot.

"Next time I am going to do better," I vowed that night. "Next time I am going to show more kindness."

I'm remembering that vow as I approach Terza Road again and ease my foot off the accelerator and consider checking in on the old farmer I abandoned to the boiling trailer. What if his brother never showed up? It's possible I could maybe find the tractor path with my high beams. I can feel the girl's ghost in the back seat watching me as my cab slows down for a few seconds before speeding up again. Sorry, ghost girl, but all I care about right now is what drink I'm going to concoct before passing out on my couch to dream about flat tires and tailgaters and three-eyed hitchhikers. It's late in the day and the tank of human kindness has run dry. As I pass the turnoff, I can't help but imagine the old man alone in that dark trailer. For all I know there's a skeleton of him sitting in that metal chair by now. For all I know the grasshoppers got him.

# IDIOT SON

*I'm kind of bummed because I'm missing right now, even as we speak, my favorite cultural train wreck:* The Tonight Show with Jay Leno. *I'm like a rubbernecker, man. Every night it's the crash of fucking metal when that show starts. Me and my friends have a little office pool wondering exactly which episode and which guest is gonna be on the night Jay finally puts a 9 mm in his mouth and blows his Dorito-shilling head off his fucking body. . . . Good God, what have I done with my life? BOOM! His brain splews out, forming an NBC peacock on the wall behind him—'cause he's a company man to the bitter fucking end.*

*It all started when he did the Doritos commercial. Here's the deal, folks. You do a commercial, you're off the artistic roll call forever. End of story, okay? You're another corporate fucking shill, you're another whore at the capitalist gangbang, and if you do a commercial there's a price on your head, everything you say is suspect, and every word that comes out of your mouth is now*

*like a turd falling into my drink. Selling Doritos on fucking TV.
. . . You don't got enough money, you fucking whore? You gotta
sell snacks to fucking bovine America now? "Hi everyone, I'm Jay
Leno. Anyone remember when I was funny? Here, eat Doritos.
They're good."*

Bill Hicks, quoted above, is buried in Mississippi, a state I'm pretty
sure he loathed even though both his parents hailed from here and in
that sense he is one of us—or at least we have custody. I think about
Hicks's stand-up comedy a lot—maybe too much—I'm OCD among
other maladies—and also, weirdly, I think about his grave, which I
imagine to be neglected save for a scattering of cigarette butts, a few
flying saucers blinking overhead, and some dirty magazines blowing
between headstones. Hicks is buried among my mother's people in
Greene County, and I have this strange desire to visit his grave and
leave him a pack of Marlboro Reds.

I'm halfway home from the Delta and thinking about Hicks, two
months younger than me yet twenty-five years dead, when the
Bluetooth rings inside my brain, and I know it's Stella, who calls me
most every return leg to treat me as her pet psychoanalyst. How to
describe these calls? Typically they involve a suicide mix of business
paranoia (Uber stealing our contact information is her latest worry,
but she's also suspicious of the flat tire I had a few days ago because
another of our drivers had a flat last week, and putting two and two
together she concludes it must be Rock Away Taxi, run by one of her
ex-employees, sabotaging our fleet). Eventually the conversation
turns to her complaints against her drivers: Danny has been charging
outlandish fees for round trips, Zeke is refusing to take any payment
besides cash, Kirby has optimistically invited a young PhD candidate

into a threesome with his wife and himself, Sam continues to make moves on any black woman who enters his cab; this is followed by a list of injected errands I have to run this week—getting keys made and side-tripping on my own gas into nearby towns to pick up money owed to Stella—followed by various explanations as to why my latest paycheck might seem to have come in short followed by a few wallows into self-pity and miscellaneous diva threats to sell the company and leave her drivers penniless followed by explanations as to why all the drivers she's hired recently have quit followed by long-winded motherly laments as to the trials of raising her jailbird son Tony, who, prior to his recent arrest in Gentry, had fled to Mississippi after a drug deal gone awry in Kansas City that had left poor Tony stabbed in the thigh and buttocks.

As far as I can tell, my purpose in these conversations—and they usually last about thirty minutes—is to make the occasional statement that is immediately contradicted (hence my image of Stella as always smoking a cantankerous cigar). No matter what I say, nope, it's dead wrong, and in fact the opposite is true, so as the call progresses I say less and less, which doesn't shorten the conversation one minute. I am Stella's sounding board just like I am the sounding board to the Borghost of racist lunatics who frequent my cab.

Stella, I should point out, has been couchbound ever since breaking her leg when a deer leapt through her windshield while she was on her way home from Mass. It was right after this wreck that she received her first prescription for opioids, which she discovered mixed great with booze.

At the end of today's conversation, I hang up exhausted and then crack open another Red Bull to stay awake. Red Bull should be sponsoring my cab the way they do race cars and those daredevils in wingsuits. As I sip my tasty energy drink, its label held toward the car camera, I'm still mulling over what Stella said, specifically the question she asked right before we hung up. Trying to sound casual, she'd asked if I'd heard from Tony recently.

"Have you seen—have you heard anything from Tony lately?"

"Tony?" I replied, my heart sinking at the mention of her son's name. "I thought he was under—I thought he was back in Kansas City?"

"He is. I'm just wondering. We're not speaking—not since the last time I fired him—and he always liked you. He said y'all were friends."

"Friends?"

"Just let me know if you hear from him, okay? I gotta go—gettin' calls."

With that, she hung up.

"Friends?" I repeated. "He said we were . . . friends?"

Let me describe this idiot son to you. He's not an adult, even though he's mid-thirties and has three kids by some long-suffering woman he calls his baby mama. Tony has a cop-shaved head of black fur that tops off at six two. Like the overgrown chimp he greatly resembles, he is muscular with long arms and legs and almost no trunk, as if he's composed only of limbs. His clothes are modeled on prison attire, and he often uses the phrase *my nigga* in referring to me, a man two decades older than him and equally white.

I first met Tony inside a taxicab being driven by Horace. Horace comes in around three fifty, which is remarkable in that he only has four teeth. To maintain this weight-to-tooth ratio he has to nibble constantly. Being a supervisor means Horace dispatches on afternoons when it's just the two of us, and during this time he'll send me every shit run—every established crazy, deadbeat, hood, or stink bomb—while he sits back in his SUV awaiting some lucrative five-person pickup to stir him to life.

He'll happily back me up five, six runs while he's sucking his way through a styrofoam nest of chicken wings.

We were in Horace's Suburban on our way to an employee meeting on the day I met Tony. As part of a plan devised by Stella, Horace had picked up Tony under false pretenses and was now forcing him to attend the employee meeting. The whole time they were arguing about this, I was in the back seat watching with a mixture of revulsion and fascination as Tony picked his nose nonstop. In my whole life I'd never seen anybody radiate idiocy so brilliantly. I didn't know he was Stella's son at the time and assumed he was another driver, but all I knew for certain was that for the last ten minutes this guy had not stopped picking his nose, that is, until the moment Horace introduced us—this is Tony, Stella's son—at which point Tony exhumed his hand and extended it toward the back seat for me to shake.

"Tony," he said.

In the months that followed, Tony became the bane of my existence. Looking back at it, I'm not sure how I survived Tony tagging along in my cab day after day. Have I ever had a happier moment than the morning I was informed he'd been arrested and shipped back to Kansas City to await trial? After hearing that news I'd danced my coffee mug across the living room. I had yet to learn what he'd been arrested for, but I hoped it was something bad, something that would send him away for life without parole.

"Friends?" I muttered again.

Even Stella had warned me about Tony. On the day she was driving me to the courthouse to pick up my taxi ID card, she'd mentioned, "By the way, my son Tony dispatches some mornings. He's an idiot."

Stella—I'd guess early sixties—had fashioned her black hair that morning into a banged jitterbug haircut and was speeding us downtown inside a blue Camaro that resembled a giant metal frog muscle. Whenever I'm around Stella I'm surprised that I like her. It's the phone Stella I dislike, the business Stella, the manipulative Stella, the lying Stella, the drunk or hungover Stella, the one always jerking me around with side trips while allowing my ball joints to decay and my brakes to fester, the one who makes all those careless bank errors in her favor.

As promised, her idiot son did attempt to dispatch some mornings, but Tony's innate laziness coupled with his temper got him fired about once a month. All the drivers would rejoice every time Stella fired Tony, although she invariably hired him back the next month. When I first started driving for All Saints, Tony dispatched from Kansas City, but then he got stabbed during the drug deal and was suddenly hiding out from the police inside his mom's house in Gentry. Not that I knew he was hiding out. None of the drivers knew Tony was on the lam. Well, Horace—one of our supervisors—might have known (he keeps his cards close), but I certainly didn't. Had I known Tony was a fugitive, I'd never have taken him on all those drug runs.

While hiding from the law at his mom's house, he would call me every morning to demand I bring him cigarettes or give him rides. He always told me he'd pay me later or to put it on his account, which Stella never paid. (Stella happily aided and abetted Tony in ripping off her drivers.) I had to deal with Tony every day, sometimes for hours on end. For months I put off standing up to him. I needed the job, and it was easier to be bullied, I felt, than to have a conflict with the boss's son.

Like many idiots Tony was fond of giving advice, a constant stream of wisdom directed at me as I drove him to the various projects orbiting Gentry and then waited outside drug houses idling in the incredibly conspicuous Town Car. The neighbors watering their coffee-can gardens stared at me balefully as I sat there thinking, *c'mon, idiot, c'mon*. To make matters worse, Tony had, during one afternoon run, admitted to me in front of my car camera that he was scoring drugs. After establishing this, he made a call to the drug dealer whose house we were parked outside.

"No, I'm the white guy, the white Tony," he corrected the dealer. "The white guy with Lil' Kane, remember? The one who owns the taxi company? Just look out the window you'll recognize me."

He rolled down the front passenger window—the only one that worked—and stared at the house Kilroy-style until the phone rang again, and then he went inside. I waited and fumed until twenty minutes later when Tony came loping toward my cab.

"Let's get out of here," he said.

I did so while glancing backward to see if anyone was chasing us.

"That's it, Tony," I told him once we were clear of the project. "I'm done with this shit."

But, as I was complaining, Tony misunderstood me—as idiots often do. He thought I was scared about us venturing into the projects (something I did every hour of every day with or without him). Tony therefore took it upon himself to deliver a civil-rights lecture in which I was informed that black people were just like us. As beautiful as it was, I had to interrupt.

"Tony, I'm not afraid of black people, I'm afraid of cops. We are obviously doing drug deals—everybody in that neighborhood knew it. We have advertising for your mother's company on the sides of this car, meaning it could be confiscated during an arrest, meaning I would have no job, and since you've already confessed to scoring drugs in front of my camera we could both be arrested. I'm like a what's-it, an accomplice. Seriously, what the fuck?"

At first he'd been so snapshot shocked at me standing up to him that he couldn't respond. A look of classic cartoon stupidity overtook his face.

"That camera doesn't even work," he mumbled after a moment.

I stared at the camera while biting back a flood of emotion. I felt like a pilgrim who'd been told God is dead.

"Doesn't work? What the hell do you mean it doesn't work?"

"I think my mom asked me to fix that one."

Deftly changing the subject, Tony explained that he was the one who had forced Stella to get the cameras in the first place. He always took credit for any aspect of Stella's competence and loved to talk about how the business would be different once he took over. And it would be different. For instance, everyone without exception would quit.

"Don't change the subject, Tony. We're talking about these drug deals of yours. I'm done with that shit. Get somebody else to drive you."

"It's just pot, dude. You really need to learn to relax."

That's true, actually. I really do need to learn to relax.

"Pot?" I said instead of relaxing. "Then how come I never smell pot? I smell it on my customers all the time, but I'm sure as hell not smelling it right now."

"You want me to show you it?"

"Yeah, why don't you do that? Hold it up to the camera and smile."

I was sure it wasn't pot. And I doubted it was heroin. I'd recently worked for a heroin addict, and Tony seemed too attentively belligerent for smack. Plus he didn't drool. Cocaine then? Could Tony afford coke? No, it must be meth.

"So show me the pot, Tony."

"Fuck this. Let's get moving."

I let off the brake.

"Where we going now? I got dispatches."

"Pick 'em up. I'll just tag along till you're empty."

That's what he always did, day after day, tagged along, sometimes for hours, and it was killing me. Twenty minutes later we were driving this old church mother named Althea home from the dialysis clinic— Althea always made me take her to Wendy's before I dropped her off at the Laurel Loop Project. One morning while driving through her project together we'd spotted this legless guy who'd fallen out of his wheelchair, and the two of us had lifted him back into his chair. Althea liked riding around with me and always encouraged me to pick up other customers before I dropped her off. Twenty minutes with Tony cured her of that forever.

While Althea was in the back, Tony began telling me a story about a friend of his in prison. The story was gruesome, but it was the way he told it, with admiration and a childlike awe, that made it so bone-chilling. Months later, when I heard Tony had been arrested at his mom's house, that story was the first thing I thought about, but at the time he told it I was mostly horrified imagining Althea listening to it in the back seat.

In the story Tony told us that afternoon one of his friends had gone to Rikers and been beaten up in the shower to the point his jaw had been left jutting off his skull. While he was lying on the tile floor in this condition, the other prisoners started lining up to orally rape him. The rape part of the story took a long time to describe—Tony told it with relish—but that was the gist of what Tony shared with us while we were in line at Wendy's waiting for Althea's post-dialysis bacon cheeseburger. It wasn't clear to me exactly what Tony saw that was so admirable in this story, but telling it clearly delighted him, and even while listening to him I kept thinking, *man, that's where you are headed, that shower room.*

"Friends?" I mouth one last time inside a chain of yawns.

Beethoven is putting me to sleep so I switch over to Big K.R.I.T. and then suddenly remember something that might qualify in Tony's primate brain as an act of friendship between us. He'd started dating this woman in Gentry—he'd met her online—and the remarkable thing about Cheryl was that she seemed normal and attractive and was a mother of two sweet kids, yet she was dating Tony, who might as well have had a Thug Life tattoo misspelled on his forehead. One night, while Stella was out of town, Tony invited Cheryl to the house, where he was going to cook her dinner and attempt to seduce her. I had to take him to Kroger to buy food. Then Tony asked could I come into the liquor store with him to help him pick out a ten-dollar bottle of wine, which I did. The next day Tony felt it necessary to tell me how successful he was that night in fucking Cheryl on his mother's living room rug, a story that ended with him saying, "What sucks is I only had one condom, so we had to keep reusing it."

Is that the moment we became friends? Did we bond over me helping him buy the bottle of wine that got him laid? Is that what made him decide to become my evil sidekick? Every day he rode along with me, and it got so bad I was about to quit. Tony had even started to tag along inside the phantom rides I gave in my dreams. Is there a difference between hate and revulsion? I suspect there is, but if not, then I truly hated Tony. Each time my phone rang I prayed, *oh God please don't let it be Tony.* Then he got arrested and a bright door of joy opened inside my heart and I started to enjoy my job.

Please, God, let him go to prison forever . . .

I drift off the road onto those border bumps, which rivet me awake, then I kill the rest of the Red Bull and start to blare Big K.R.I.T., but at the moment my hand touches the volume knob—I'm right at the edge of town where the streetlights begin—I see Tony, or I think I see him. Is it actually Tony or just some kind of taurine hallucination? The Tony I see or don't see is hitchhiking on the side of the highway, and in my imagination our eyes meet for that one second I speed past him and then I check the rearview to try to make sure it wasn't him.

"No," I beg the god of rearview mirrors. "Please, not Tony. Give me any other monster."

# STARGAZING

After finishing graduate school at Syracuse, I returned to Fayetteville, Arkansas, the only place I'd ever been happy. Once there, I found a job bartending and moved into a hunting cabin perched on a hill just outside of town, and on Saturday nights I would clamber onto the roof of my cabin to watch the Razorbacks play football in the valley below. Often as not, I shared that view with a host of possum, coon, and feral cats. These critters fought and fucked gamely over dominion of my attic, and occasionally one of them fell as if electrocuted through the mailing paper I'd used to patch up the holes in the ceiling. Garter snakes kept slithering into my living room—I'd capture them inside paper bags—and every night, as soon as it got dark, hundreds of jumping spiders emerged through the floorboards. Later, when I was presumably asleep, tarantula-sized spiders toting white egg sacs ranged the walls while congregations of black widows with gleaming red hourglasses congealed above doorways inside gossamer clouds.

After my first month of rustic living, when the rutting in my attic reached a pitch too raucous to sleep beneath, I borrowed a 12-gauge shotgun from my friend Zach and staked out my backyard in hopes of assassinating the possum that had been spying on me through a missing ceiling tile in my kitchen whenever I cooked meat. On the third night of my vigil, the possum appeared and sauntered across the yard toward the woods. At first I thought it was a trick of moonlight that made the possum appear so ghostly white, but by the time I'd snuck up behind it and raised the shotgun, I was pretty sure it was an albino possum. I stood there afraid to pull the trigger. I knew a gunshot this late would scare the hell out of the old man who lived in the cabin below mine. Also, I'd never shot anything in my life.

As I hesitated, the possum turned and started ambling directly toward me to the point I had to use the shotgun to prod it away. When I did that, the possum pivoted and resumed its march toward the woods. Right before it reached the trees, I pulled the trigger. The deafening blast severed the creature in half, but the head and front paws kept clawing forward. Holding that shotgun, feeling the ache in my shoulder and watching the tattered half of a moonlit possum swimming forward on dark grass, I felt as if I had reinvented myself.

A few days later, my friend Zach and I were up on the roof of my cabin watching the Razorbacks play in the valley below—we could only see half the football field—and I was telling Zach about the other time I had hideously murdered a possum—not the one I'd just shot. Mostly I was doing this to get Zach's mind off Alma, the Cajun girl who'd just broken Zach's Cajun heart. Zach was the most lovesick person I'd ever seen. He was a poet and I guess that's an occupational hazard.

"There's a witch in this story, Zach," I said, trying to bait him away from the suicide jump he seemed to be contemplating off the roof.

"I love her, man. Even though she gave me VD." He sighed before adding, "We should run more slants."

Zach had been a high-school quarterback back in Mamou. During his junior year there, he'd fallen in love with a 14-year-old girl, the only blonde person in the history of the town, apparently, and Alma was indeed model beautiful and model trustworthy. Prior to their recent breakup, Zach at age twenty-five had never even had a sip of alcohol, but within days of Alma fleeing with her new lover to California, Zach was swigging tequila and passing joints with me. Set against that star-spackled sky, the updraft of the highway cloverleaf competing with the stadium roar, he cut a forlorn figure with that long, luxurious black hair worthy of a good-guy wrestler. Like Alma, Zach had been born anomalous into an overweight, cancer-fraught gene pool unaccustomed to offspring of unearthly beauty.

"A real witch," I insisted.

"A *sorcière*?"

"Yeah. Well, a witch. And not some bullshit new age witch, either. I'm talking a spell-casting fuck-things-up witch."

"She stole my credit card. And used it to buy two hundred bucks' worth of French underwear for that bastard who gave me VD. But I still love her. I can't help it. We need to stop running laterally."

Zach and I had become friends as undergrads. Back then I'd lusted terribly after Alma, so much so that once at Syracuse I even found a girlfriend who kinda-sorta resembled her. Leslie was supposed to join me in Arkansas once she got her degree, but I'd spent that afternoon drafting a letter breaking up with her. I'd never been good at long-term relationships, but how can you change something like that about yourself? How can you make yourself sexually attracted to somebody you've slept with hundreds of times already when the planet is filled with beautiful women walking around half naked who you've never slept with once? Sometimes I wondered if I'd ever been in love, really in love. I'd certainly never been anywhere near as miserable over a woman as Zach was that night.

That would change soon enough, but I had no inkling of it that night on the roof.

"How I met this witch," I said to Zach, "my friend Michael Gullet and I were at this bar. You never met Michael. He was, well, like you, a dandy poet, but he was even more vain than you are. When we went fishing, he used to knot the ends of his shirt over his abs. Anyway, Michael was a good guy when he was sober. Which was never. And he was a horrible, horrible person whenever he was drunk—like the worst drunk in the world. A nightmare. So one night the two of us were at this bar, the whatever bar. I'd never been there before. Michael wanted to go there. I drove us because Michael had about twelve DUIs, and once we got to the bar, I ended up talking to this woman, kinda giving her shit because she was wearing black lipstick and black nail polish and told me she was a witch, a road witch. No, wait, not a road witch, a car witch."

"A car witch," Zach repeated in a wan voice that let me know his mind was far away and suffering terribly.

"Right. Because all her spells fucked with people's cars. So while I'm talking up this car witch—she was definitely cute—I think her name was Mayfern—or maybe that was the girl she was with—and I'm kinda teasing her about being a car witch, and as I'm doing this Michael is at the far end of the bar frantically trying to get my attention without Mayfern noticing. He's like landing invisible airplanes, gesturing me toward the bathroom, and he seems seriously freaked out about something. And I'm trying to ignore him because, you know, I'm chatting up this hot witch. Hand me that, huh?"

"Mayfern," Zach mused while passing me the half-empty bottle of tequila we'd opened before kickoff.

"Right. Mayfern. So finally I go to the bathroom, and there's Michael, and he's sweating bullets, telling me we gotta get out of here, and whatever you do don't talk to that chick, she's dangerous, man, she's *a real fucking witch!* He's like panicked."

"Mayfern," Zach said again.

"Yeah. So Mayfern and Michael had some history, and he was clearly freaked out by Mayfern's powers. Me, I wanted to go home with Mayfern and see what that was like, so I blew him off and went back to the bar and shot the shit with Mayfern and kept teasing her about being a car witch, because I was like, a car witch? Seriously? What kind of a witch is that? I wasn't being mean, just flirting or whatever, but apparently I was getting on her nerves—go figure—and the whole time I'm getting on her nerves, Michael's still across the bar from us making all these horror-movie faces. I'd never seen him scared of anything, but, whatever, I was drunk, who cares, right? Pass the bottle."

"You've already got it."

"I know I got it. That was a literary allusion. Where'd my lighter go?"

"On your knee."

"Ah. Here, hold this." I relit the joint and exhaled as the crowd below us cheered a Razorback first down. "At some point I must have really pissed Mayfern off—that becomes indisputable later—because she gets mad, makes some vague threat about my car, I laugh it off, and then a little later Michael and I leave. At first Michael won't even get in my Datsun, because he knows she's a car witch. And once we're inside, he makes me go like twenty miles per hour and starts chewing me out. I drop him off, he slams the door—very unlike Michael, but, whatever—I drive home—no wreck, no DUI—I pull into the driveway, go inside, and pass out."

"Where's the possum come in?"

"We're getting to the possum, Zach. We're there, actually. The next morning I get up hungover as hell and stagger around making coffee and carry the mug outside to the front steps, and while I'm sitting there blowing on my coffee I start hearing this groaning noise, like this long ghost moan, and holy shit I look around and damned if there isn't an animal of some sort—a fucking possum, Zach—half squashed under the front tire of my Datsun. I didn't even notice the possum at the time, but obviously I'd hit it the night before when I pulled into the driveway. So I'm like, yeah, Mayfern, fuck! But Mayfern's just getting started, man. Here, hit this. It'll make you feel better."

"No it won't." But he took the joint anyway. After he quit coughing from it, he asked, "Was it an albino possum?"

"No. It was just a regular possum, my first possum ever, and it turns out holy God they've got these incredible fangs, like vipers, and when they hiss at you it's like somebody set a house cat on fire, and this possum had veins and turds pouring out its mouth from being half run over, but it was still, you know, very much alive and extremely pissed off. And I don't know what to do with it. I need to put it out of its misery, but how? Then I notice a shovel on my neighbor's porch, and I think, ah, the shovelhead coup de grace. So I sneak over and steal the shovel—the neighbor already hates my guts because my cat keeps attacking his kid—don't ever buy a pet-store cat, they're all psychopaths—and I slink back into my yard and start whacking the possum over the head with the shovel. It's like seven in the morning, right? My coffee's still cooling on the steps, and here I am hatcheting this poor possum with a shovelhead, and every time I hit the possum it just goes crazy. And this motherfucker will not die. I hit it like two dozen times, aiming at various judo deathblow spots, but nothing changes except its hissing gets more and more satanic. My arms are getting tired, and I'm about to throw up, and while I'm standing there hacking away, I'm also kinda imagining myself being spied on out the kitchen window by the neighbor who hates my guts. Finally I give up and just lean against the shovel panting. My brain's one giant heartbeat by now, but eventually it occurs me, duh, I should just get back inside the car and finish running over the damn thing. Let the car finish the job."

"Uh-uh, man. That car's bad gris-gris."

"I got no choice. I've got the world's worst hangover now. I find my keys and finish running over the possum. But, thing is, it was already crushed along that tread path, so it doesn't really do much extra damage. I get out, look, and the possum starts screaming at me like, MOTHERFUCKER LEAVE ME ALONE!, like, WHAT DID I EVER DO TO YOU? And I stagger back into the car and back over him, get out, and it's the same thing—YOUR MOTHER SUCKS COCKS IN HELL!—and after a while I've run over the possum like four times and crushed every part of its body except the head, but that head is still alive and screaming bloody murder, and finally, I dunno, I'm defeated, I just give up, get out of the car—I'm shaking—and then I do the worst thing I've ever done in my life. I'm so hungover, but still that's no excuse for what I did next. Man, drink this so I don't finish it all. We're a team, Zach, like the Razorbacks."

He took a pull of tequila and winced it down.

"What'd you do that was so bad?" he asked after he'd quit shuddering.

"Uh? Oh, God, what I did." I paused to light the joint again. "Here, trade. What I did was, I used the shovel to scoop up the possum. It looked like a bloody pancake with a possum head sticking out the top, but it was still hissing at me as I walked it across the street like this to an apartment complex and tossed it inside their dumpster. So now the poor possum's dying alone inside a grave of stinking garbage. Man, I felt like shit for doing that. I should have run over its head, but I just couldn't. Every time I tried, I got, like, possum fever. It's not a cigarette, Zach. Pinch it."

"So Mayfern struck."

He passed me the joint and I passed him the bottle.

"Exactly. Don't mess with Mayfern. Lesson fucking learned."

"That's really the worst thing you've ever done?"

"Huh?"

"You said that was the worst thing you ever did."

"Oh. No. Of course not."

"So what's the worst thing you've ever done?"

"The worst thing I've ever done? Jesus." I hit the joint and then studied it. "Well, Zach, I'll tell you. I once had this amazing girl-friend who everyone loved and admired, just a stellar person, and then one day I gave her VD and stole her credit card to buy this other chick I was fucking a whole passel of Victoria's Secret lingerie. Here."

He took the joint and a moment later blew smoke up at the stars.

"I love her, man," he whispered. "She's probably in Hollywood right now sucking cock in front of some video camera wearing the under-wear she bought with my credit card so she can pay that asshole's rent who gave me gonorrhea. But I can't help it. I still love her."

I studied him a minute. Like trying to make sense of a different species.

"Zach, maybe we should go to that whatever bar right now. Maybe a night with Mayfern is what you really need."

"I'm not messing with no *sorcière*."

"You might change your mind once you see her. She was really hot. That black lipstick was killing me. I'd never slept with a witch. Well, good witches, I guess—or women who perceived themselves to be good witches—but not, you know, a legitimately hex-firing bad witch. She'd probably be incanting like crazy the whole time—it'd be awesome."

The stadium crowd started booing at something we couldn't see.

"Was it really an albino possum?" Zach asked. "The one you shot with my 12-gauge?"

"You know it was. You saw its body. Bodies."

"Yeah, but it just looked sort of dirty white."

"It was an albino possum, I swear. You should have seen those spooky pink eyes."

But I don't think Zach even heard what I'd said. He just kept staring up at the sky, probably hoping to spot a falling star he could cast a wish upon to bring Alma back home so she could make him suffer wretchedly forever. I looked up at the stars too and started searching for UFOs. Ever since I was a kid, back when that famous flying saucer landed in Pascagoula and kidnapped those two fisher-men, I'd had this obsession with looking for UFOs. Mayfern and I had even discussed UFOs that night at the bar. She'd told me that gray aliens kept abducting her to steal her ovaries. And that's what I was thinking about while Zach kept searching for a falling star, about Mayfern picking me up in a flying saucer and us having wild incantation sex inside it while this circle of eggheaded aliens watched us go at it.

"I love her, man."

That startled me. For a minute I'd forgotten where I was.

"Look at it this way, Zach," I said. "Think about that story I just told you. About the car witch and the non-albino possum. Think of that story as an allegory."

"An allegory?"

"Yeah. In this allegory, Alma is me, okay? I represent Alma. I'm Alma with a shovel. Now guess who you are?"

He squinted like someone spying into the distance and whispered, "I'm the possum."

"That's right, Zach. I'm Alma, and you're the possum."

At that moment I spotted the falling star Zach had been hoping for and stole his wish. I wished for Leslie to break up with me before I had to break up with her, but what I was really thinking about when I made my wish was making love to Mayfern inside a flying saucer with her long, black nails raking down my back as the aliens took notes.

Zach kept searching the sky while the Razorbacks tried to kick a long and desperate field goal to tie the game. I could see the kicker but not the goalpost, but I knew he'd missed from how quickly the crowd fell quiet.

"So what's Mayfern?" Zach asked.

"Huh?"

"If it's an allegory, Mayfern's got to be something, too. Or it's not an allegory."

"Oh, right." I thought that over and said, "Mayfern is God, Zach."

"God?"

"Yeah. I'm pretty sure Mayfern is God."

Zach mulled that over and after a moment shook his head and whispered, "I still love her, man. I can't help it."

It got quiet again after that, and for the longest time we both kept staring up at the stars for different reasons. Mostly I was thinking about Mayfern, but every once in a while I'd peek over at Zach. It awed me how devoted he was. And it wasn't an act, either, his grief was real, and in my own small way I felt some jealousy over his capacity to suffer love, which in turn made me recall the letter I'd written Leslie earlier that day and made me hesitant to mail it. In the end, I didn't break up with Leslie—I kept putting it off—and when she visited me over Christmas break, instead of breaking up with her I accidentally got her pregnant and we ended up moving to her hometown in Vermont, where she divorced me after three years of marriage for being a miserable fuck mired in seasonal depression. Following our divorce, I managed to stay in Burlington until my son finished high school without hurling myself pell-mell down some Black Diamond slope of doom, but it was a close call all around and even now I'm not sure how I survived it.

# MOONDOG'S TAXI

The next morning I start the day with Ozium, Beethoven, and coffee and sit for an hour parked at the town square taxi slot watching beautiful women meander to work and wondering what happened to my sex drive after I pulled that deer tick off my neck. Post-tick I tend to watch women out of nostalgia and habit. I miss lust. Lust gets you in trouble, sure, but it's great for killing time, and business being slow means hours spent staring wistfully out windows. Rain starts to fall, just hard enough to blur away faces and figures. If the rain gets really bad, the roof of my Town Car will leak directly onto my head (and nowhere else in the cab), but for now it's just a shower and nothing like the downpour required to drench me. The women passing by look like reflections of women glimpsed in puddles.

Miko was asleep, or pretending to sleep, when I got in last night, and she was still sleeping, or pretending to, when I left for work this morning. Not that her being awake would have set off any fireworks. Sometimes I think it's her own low sex drive that's infected mine—maybe it's not the tick at all. I've really got to get her out of my house, for both our sakes, but I've been putting it off for years now and it just becomes more impossible by the day. It's not a relationship we have anymore. We're hardly even roommates. We are ghosts from different dimensions who happen to overlap in our existential existences and only materialize into each other's lives to scream and spit at one another before disappearing again. Of all the types of loneliness I've endured this is by far the worst, with none of the solace of solitude and the forever feeling that even the air you exhale disapproves of you.

As to our arguments, it's always shocking how they quicken her, as if during her hibernations she's been storing up grievances and for-mulating some of the strangest theories about my psyche, and then, boom, once I say the wrong thing, the trigger gets pulled. Her theo-ries about me are astonishingly wrong—I can't even get my mind around most of them—but, on the other hand, she's just psychic enough to know how to injure me.

"Stop being psychic!" my ghost screamed at her just last week.

To which her ghost screamed back, "Stop being transparent!"

My first pickup of the morning is two meth heads at the Down-n-Out, better known as the Rebel Motel (with *rebel* pronounced as a verb by locals to create a rhyme). The Rebel is famous for murders and suicides but also for hosting art hops in which local painters appropri-ate the cell-like rooms to display their still lifes to hipsters. It's early morning as I pull into the parking lot with the sun sliding between clouds. The Rebel has fake Spanish tiles, and its parking lot mimics a traditional Mexican courtyard. All the doors are painted different colors, but the sun has weathered them so severely it's easy not to notice this. Every time I wait in the parking lot—and we get a lot of calls to the Rebel—I can't stop imagining the motel as a shootout scene in some spaghetti Western.

But today I don't have to wait. My fares must have been spying out the peephole of the room with the faded red door. Meth-head women always look the same to me, gaunt twins dressed in the dark with garage-sale leftovers. One is wearing tie-dye with jeans, the other a black Harley-Davidson tee shirt over black lycra, their gray-black hair pulled back into identical ponytails. One of the women tells me straightaway that they are being stalked by the husband of one and the son of the other—the same guy—and that they are leaving town in two days to escape certain death at his hands.

"Jase'll kill us sure," the woman brags. "That's why EverSaved is taking us to their shelter in Memphis." She pauses, then adds, "We've fallen on hard times."

I nod, avoiding eye contact in the rearview, because obviously this is leading to a reduction-of-fare plea. I am being played with misery. Knowing this, I drive tight-lipped and wary. It's a cigarette run with an extra stop at McDonald's. All cabbies hate stops, especially fast-food ones. Stops pay only two dollars each, the city law, and sometimes you have to drive miles out of your way and then wait for ten minutes guzzling gas.

Customers are always asking me how cabbies get paid. With a nervous glance to the camera recording my life, I tell them taxis work just like sharecropping used to work, and sometimes I'll even quote how Harry Crews described that arrangement: "Shares meant the owner would supply the land, fertilizer, seed, mules, harness, plows, and at harvest take half of everything that was made." With cab driving, the company supplies the car, the larger maintenance, the licensing, insurance, phones, bribes, and dispatchers. Drivers pay gas and small maintenance and come harvest split the drop. Most of Stella's drivers work at least sixty-hour weeks and don't have bank accounts or health insurance, they've never taken a vacation, and many of them don't have but three or four teeth in their skulls. (If there's one thing spectacularly clear about All Saints Taxi, it's that we don't have dental.) And if a driver falls ill or gets injured, he is royally screwed. Although he is an employee in almost every measure of the word, he is legally what's called an independent contractor, meaning he is disposable. Therefore when a cabbie picks up some meth heads at the Rebel Motel he knows all too well he is one accident away from living in the room next door to them.

Our first stop is a convenience store, which, as it turns out, doesn't have the two-for-one Luckies special my meth heads desperately need. So now we have to go to a Mobile station three miles in the opposite direction. "I coulda swore it was Chevron had that deal," one of the meth heads laments. They keep chatting me up about how great the car smells, how wonderful the AC feels. "I could take a nap back here." Telling me how handsome I am, how the women must be hitting on me all day. (Nope.) Playing me. Meth heads at their game.

At the Mobile station, Black Lycra, the mother-in-law, stays in the car while Tie-Dye runs inside, their theory being they will halve their odds of being murdered if one of them remains hidden behind my tinted windows. Meanwhile I am thinking: God, if you exist, please don't let these women get me killed. I warn myself not to intervene. They are not your people. And anyway what kind of an insane knight would take a bullet for a disease-laden meth head? I sit behind the wheel practicing my apathy while imagining a murder transpiring on the hood of the Town Car.

For the last year I've been driving the '95 ebony Lincoln, which I sometimes call the Black Widow on those days it feels like I've been eaten alive. Most everybody else in town calls my cab "Moondog's taxi"—Matt Moondowski being the first cabbie to drive it before Stella fired him for stealing or drug dealing or both or neither and I inherited the car. Topping eighteen feet, the Lincoln is one of the longest sedans in Detroit history. It's a wonderful automobile: V8, leather interior, air shocks, digital dash, with a defunct Austin Powers phone nestled inside the armrest. All the other cabbies in town drive androgynous minivans or SUVs, three-rowed suburban houses on wheels, but All Saints needs one sleek sedan low to the ground for ferrying the elderly, the crippled, and the rich. My only complaint with the Town Car, aside from its spongy brakes and piebald tires, aside from the broken ball joint that could cause a tire to fly off at any moment, aside from its rainy roof and the endless creaking and bottoming out, is that the horn doesn't work. The horn didn't work when Stella bought the car two years ago at 100,000 miles, the horn doesn't work now at 210,000, and the horn won't ever work again no matter how often I badger Stella to get it fixed. I've already been broadsided once by some bowhead playing Pokémon Go. Late at night, while falling asleep, I often remember that collision, the slow motion nobody-can-hear-you-screamness of it.

Yet every time I complain to Stella about the horn, she assures me that a good driver doesn't need one. And in some ways she's right. A horn, like an active sex drive, can get you shot or blackjacked or coldcocked or rear-ended. Not having a horn has been a constant lesson. I'm a better person for it. Yes, a good driver doesn't really need a horn, that is, until that moment he's about to be flung through his windshield into the Great Unknown. Then they come in handy, horns do.

"We're leaving for Memphis in two days," Black Lycra tells me from the back seat. "Unless Jason finds us first. He's shit-bird crazy, that boy. Come back from Iraq with the post-traumatic fever and wound up in Parchman for cracking Cindy's skull open with his motorcycle helmet. Now that he's out, he speaks in tongues all the time."

She makes a series of nonsensical gurgling sounds in imitation of her son's dementia. When she's done, she adds, "Trust me, it ain't Jesus pourin' out that boy."

I nod again but don't otherwise reply. Why bother? They'll be gone in twenty minutes. That's the beauty of the job. No matter how weird it gets, or how terrible it smells, they will be gone soon. And usually I am friendly. I like my job. I like interacting with strange lives however briefly. Except when I'm being played by meth heads.

When we get to McDonald's, I tell them the back window is glued shut so they'll have to go inside to order, but they don't want to risk it. The drive-through is much safer, they insist.

"He sees us here, he'll kill us sure."

"And that boy loves his McDonald's."

"I wonder who he'll kill first? Probably you, huh, Cindy?"

"Shit, he'll kill whoever's damn closest and you know it, girl—pardon my French."

"It wasn't me set him on fire."

"But it was your idea to. You're the one said it would drive the devil out him."

I pull in line and tell them I'll order for them.

"Hey, just so y'all know, it's two dollars a stop, plus twenty bucks for two people round-trip. But if this stop takes more than ten minutes then I got to start charging you a dollar a minute. I got regulars waiting to go to work."

And that much is true. Day shift is mostly regulars, meaning people who have structured their lives around cab rides. A bad day cabbie can get people fired, can ruin their lives. After explaining the rates, I make a big to-do over starting the stopwatch app on my mounted cell phone. I'm hoping they'll abandon the McDonald's stop. Like Stella, I spend a lot of energy lying and manipulating.

"A dollar a minute! But EverSaved told us y'all had a flat fare."

EverSaved is a local church association that sometimes hides abused women from their stalkers inside seedy motels. I've taken at least ten women to EverSaved's Memphis shelter, so I know, in spite of not wanting to know, the dire fate awaiting these meth heads.

"Everybody has a flat fare," I tell them. "That's the city law. Trust me, I'm losing money here."

We haggle. Eventually I cave in and tell them I'll do the whole run, stops and all, for the twenty. The meth-head special.

There are four cars ahead of us in line, one of them a church van. I am running the AC full blast, eighty-two degrees outside at 7:10 AM, the Town Car butt-chugging the gas, a new text message pinging in every few minutes now as people migrate to work. Stella's last text contains four misspelled words, two vexing autocorrects, and an arbitrary mix of emojis, letters, and numbers that makes it appear vaguely Egyptian. I take this to mean she has an especially bad hangover. Staring into this message I begin to worry it's going to be one of those days. I never believed in astrology before driving a cab, but now I often find myself wondering if the stars don't show up for work as hungover and misaligned as Stella does.

Superstition. A few decades ago, back when I was a budding young writer with a swanky Brooklyn girlfriend, back before I went cold on the page and never finished that second novel I'd already been paid for, I used to live on the third floor of a tenement in the Lower East Side. Orchard Street, in the old Bargain District, was filled with luggage stores and hawkers screaming out bargains. These hawkers had a belief that the first sale of the morning dictated the day. So if you were the first customer through the door, you could wrangle a healthy discount. Likewise I tend to regard my first fare of the day as a tell, a hint as to what cards the stars might be holding. And right now I suspect it's a full house of craven meth heads, spit-cupped bigots, shape-shifted aliens, suicide ex-cons, and one-eyed vomiting perverts.

I risk a glance into the rearview and ask, "Hey, what did you say his name was? The guy stalking y'all?"

"Jason," Tie-Dye replies cheerfully.

"Jason? Like in the horror movie?"

"Yeah. Was he the one with the hockey mask?" Black Lycra wants to know.

"No, he's the one sprung out the lake, dummy. I damn near shit my pants."

I glance around the parking lot.

"So how often does Jason eat at McDonald's?"

"Like every damn meal."

"That boy was raised off the dollar menu."

"Huh," I say.

A burnished black motorcycle pulls into the line behind us thereby blocking any hope of escape. The driver keeps revving the engine maliciously. I can't see his hog very well, but I can tell it's a Harley from the machine-gun cadence. I put on my knockoff aviators and glare over the imaginary murder still unfolding on my hood. The line is not moving. Therefore I am not moving. Trying to distract myself from my need to nudge forward, from my desire to lay on a horn that doesn't exist, I open my chessboard app to see if my son has put me into check yet—I haven't beaten him in months—but he hasn't moved. Still asleep in Vermont.

Three cars to go . . . the church van taking forever.

*C'mon*, I mutter to myself for the thousandth hundredth millionth time: *C'mon, motherfucker, c'mon, c'mon . . .*

There's a type of Tourette's, unique to hackies, called "a yellow mind." Due to this malady cabbies drive around autocorrecting the world with a cuss-filled stream of consciousness. Quick-tempered, thin-skinned, a loogie of obscene complaints resting viscously on our tongues, we didn't start off this way. No, it's the job that yellows the mind. It's the bubbas in monster trucks who don't use turn signals because they consider them to be effeminate, it's Sunday drivers and suicidal pedestrians, it's the endless convoys of construction vehicles on their way to build more condominiums for the so-called students to throw up inside. You flip off the red light because you know it's not really inanimate—it's possessed—there's an evil spirit trapped inside every traffic light—and in spite of all your well-meaning resolutions you once again find yourself pounding the steering wheel and cursing the endless taunts of traffic. Then, late at night, unable to sleep, you replay all the tantrums you threw in front of the camera mounted next to your rearview, that single eye peering ceaselessly into your soul. You don't understand exactly how that camera works—it some- how communicates with a metal box in your trunk—occasionally your supervisor downloads that information into a metal box in his trunk—and because you don't understand how anything works, you worry that Stella can watch you whenever the whim hits, maybe that's what she does all day, maybe she's smoking a cigar right now while watching you flail in traffic flipping off for the hundredth time that *Exorcist* of a red light at the corner of Finch and Coleman.

The church van starts to pull away, but then its driver discovers his order has been shorted and backs up while laying on the horn. Meanwhile two more text messages bing in. A rare four-passenger pickup, twenty-five bucks minimum, cancels on me. The other message wants to know where the hell I am. I use voice recognition to reply so as to guilt-trip my meth heads and let them know they are making honest people late for work. I do that kind of stuff too often. There is a Puritan inside me whom I despise. But he's always there in his black hat and square belt buckle holding a turkey in his arms. I'd happily kill that little bastard if I could, but, being part of my country, part of my psyche, this inner pilgrim possesses me at will and sets me to screaming at all the things he hates and then later reproves me of the childish tantrums he inspired.

This morning I get off easy. In today's episode of this perpetual horror movie the serial-killer son-in-law doesn't spring out of a lake or through the McDonald's drive-through window. And, much to my surprise, the meth-head twins produce a crisp twenty without further arbitration in the motel parking lot. I go ahead and give them a five back and tell them best of luck in Memphis.

"Hey, maybe you'll end up taking us to the shelter," Tie-Dye says.

I try not to cringe. The Memphis shelter looks like some bunker they stored ammunition inside during World War I. I've even heard rumors it's a brothel.

"Can we request you?" she asks.

"Sure," I say. Then she asks my name. Although I'm tempted to lie, I tell her the truth. "It's Lou."

"Sweet Lou," Black Lycra says and winks at me.

With that, they walk to their red door and wave goodbye to me like *Titanic* passengers. Not to be too confessional here, but I've been inside those rooms and stood over those beds wondering how many people had committed suicide on the far side of the mattress. I force a smile and wave back from behind tinted glass as their door swings shut.

Then they are gone.

# SHIT JOBS

If I were rich I'd find the darkest paradise on earth and build the biggest telescope I could afford and hang up my hammock and never work again, but I'm not rich so instead I will keep moving from shit job to shit job until I die. Because Stella had screwed up the paperwork, it took months to get me licensed to drive a cab in Gentry, and by the time I was approved I'd already memorized every pothole in town. Part of the reason I overprepared for the taxi job was panic. For the first time in my life I'd started getting fired. I'd bartended in a sushi joint and gotten fired for being half deaf and prone to back spasms. I managed a karaoke club that also hosted teenage body-paint raves and got fired for refusing to do heroin with the skeevy owner. I got hired to stand along roadside ditches at 2:00 AM aiming night-vision goggles at passing vehicles in order to determine if the terrified people inside were wearing seat belts, and I got fired from that gig for sloppy paperwork. I smuggled winter vegetables inside a gutted prisoners van from south Louisiana into north Mississippi and got fired for screaming obscenities at my boss about the illegal sixteen-hour driving stints that were going to get me crushed to death by boxes of cucumbers. I taught an adjunct class at the local university and found the alt-right student body disheartening but stuck it out in order to achieve my dream of teaching Shakespeare, at which I proved heartbreakingly incompetent. I had done all these jobs poorly, I felt. There were times I could have been more diligent. For instance, during the night-vision-goggle gig, I spent far too much time scanning the stars for UFOs.

I'm parked at the town square reliving all the moments I got fired when I get dispatched back to the hospital, this time the ER side. I drive there slowly, almost begging people to tailgate me, luring them in to flip them off. I don't want to go back to the hospital. For one thing, Chloe will probably be there, and right now I feel too feral to be around her. Who the hell would ever want to date a cabdriver? Not even in movies do women fall in love with cabbies. No, nobody loves us.

While still awaiting my taxi license to be approved, I'd started motoring around town on my Vespa drawing maps. Earlier that year I'd crashed that scooter into a tree and broken my clavicle in five places. Sporting a new titanium collarbone (you could count the five screwheads through my skin), I backfired around Gentry setting to memory the names of each business, dorm, sorority house, and seedy motel. During these jaunts, I was purposely emulating the taxi certification program in London known as the Knowledge, in which would-be cabbies have to recite the location of every business in the city and the best route to get there depending on the time of day. Entire memory systems had been devised to pass that test. Luckily there is a tradition of memory systems in London that goes back to Shakespeare. Back then, there were men who could recite the entire New Testament. And the funny thing about the memory system used to hoard the life of Jesus into a lobe of the human brain is that the technique was purposely obscene, a memory palace of lewd cartoons, each disgusting detail a trigger to a follow-up concept inside a domino fall of re-remembrance, the basic premise being that the more pornographic a detail the easier it is to recall. Soon my entire town became a map of crude cartoons, but within weeks of starting the job I was the fastest cabbie in town.

I leave the car idling and walk inside the ER and do the paperwork, then I stand there recalling all the hospital waiting rooms I've slept inside for weeks and months on end. Comas run in my family. And unless Stella fixes my brakes, I'm pretty sure I'm next in line. As I stand there imagining myself arriving in an ambulance, Chloe walks over and gives me a grin. Like me, she's tall and thin and has long dark hair and a long face—we could be brother and sister. She reminds me a little of the wife in *The Shining*, except Chloe is older and prettier, her wide brown eyes less nervous, her grin more wicked.

"Did they tell you she just got out of prison?" she asks.

Sometimes prisoners with medical conditions have to be released through the hospital.

"No. They never tell me anything. What was she in for?"

"You'll know once you see her."

"Oh. Well, where am I taking her?"

"Grampus Lake. She owns a camper there. Except her husband, who also just got out of prison, might be staying in it now. They're half divorced and hate each other, so God only knows what'll happen once y'all show up."

"Lovely. Anything else I should know?"

"Just keep an eye on your kitty, sweetie."

"Yeah. I usually put it in the trunk when I get a hospital run."

"That bad, huh?"

"No, not always. It's just one less thing to worry about."

"I bet you got some stories."

"Nothing that would impress an ER nurse."

"I'm not so sure." She gives me the grin—it never fails to floor me—then adds, "Maybe we should trade horror stories over a beer sometime and see who has the worst ones."

This catches me off guard, a clear opening to ask her out, and of course I fumble it with a long pan of silence before finally managing to cough out, "The worst ones are the best."

The statement just sits there in all its nonsensicalness until Chloe raises her long arm and says, "There she blows. Miss Pamela."

A remarkably thin woman with blanched hair is being wheeled out of a nearby room. I study Pamela a moment and then whisper, "It's almost like they're some kind of alien species we have to take care of."

Chloe laughs and says, "I wish they'd go back to their own planet."

We say goodbye and I walk outside still kicking myself over the missed opportunity to ask her out. An orderly is situating my passenger into the back seat. Pamela has long straight hair that is mostly white but with hints of the blonde who first flirted with meth. Her abducted eyes are pale blue, her arms sticks, her hands claws, her nails chewed. I'd guess fifty, but who knows with them, right?

"I am so glad to be the hell out of there," she tells me as we pull away from the hospital. "Pardon my damn French."

"Grampus Lake, huh?" I reply in the voice I reserve for meth heads.

The campground is about twenty miles away, meaning an eighty-dollar haul, of which I will pocket half minus gas whenever Stella decides to pay up.

"I just hope my camper's still there. My ex-husband knows where I hide the key."

And already I know that camper is not going to be there.

"Maybe you should call him? You only get this one free ride."

"The asshole won't pick up. Pardon my Spanish. Anyway I got nowhere else to go."

Nowhere else to go, I think. Where do you go when you got nowhere else to go? Well, you call a cab.

"Hey, is that Bigfoot?"

"Yeah. It's pine-scented."

"Never seen one." Then she points to my UFO air freshener and adds, "But I used to see those little bastards all the time."

"Were you on meth?" I want to ask but don't. Instead I say, "I've never seen a saucer, I just keep seeing those triangle ones."

"I've only seen the saucers. When I was a kid they used to follow me around. Hey, is that Shakespeare?"

"Yeah. It's Shakespeare-mint."

"Huh. I've always wanted to read him. But I never will."

Halfway to Grampus Lake we hit a line of thunderstorms and the car starts leaking rain onto my head.

"That's kinda sad how it only lands on you," Pamela notes.

We drive to the reservoir and start snaking along the low roads beneath the dam. There are puddles everywhere, but the sun is out again and the road is already steaming. I'm still thinking about Chloe—but also about breaking up with Miko. As we approach the campground, Pamela begins praying out loud. *Please let my camper be there, Jesus. Please, please, please, Jesus.* And I know, know in my bones, that camper isn't going to be there.

We round a corner and she whispers, "Oh God, it's gone."

I stop the car and close my eyes a moment. Goddamnit Jesus, I think. Would it have fucking killed you to give this poor lady her camper?

Pamela reaches forward and begins clawing at my right arm. Climbing it almost. I have to fight the urge to shirk her off.

"Please, sir, let's drive around some. He mighta hid it in another spot."

So we drive around the campground for twenty minutes. Then we drive around some county roads where she thinks the camper might be hidden, but of course it isn't there either. Eventually I pull into the parking lot of El Pollo Loco. Right behind the restaurant is a billboard advertising something about hepatitis C.

"Pamela," I say, "I'm sorry, but I'm not getting paid for any of this. I gotta take you back to the hospital, I guess. Unless you want to stay here."

"Please, can you take me to Pontotoc. Please. I've got nothing."

"Pontotoc? That's like a hundred and twenty dollars from here. Who's gonna pay me for that?"

"There's a man there will. I know he will. Mr. Calvin will. He's a bail bondsman. I promise he will."

It's about the quickest lie ever conjured. I try to imagine any man happy enough to see this meth head to pay me a buck twenty on delivery.

"He lives in the woods off Highway 9. Please." Pamela is clutching my elbow again, pulling me into the back seat like an octopus into her lair. "I got nowhere else."

I imagine myself, briefly, being robbed in the woods off Highway 9 by Mr. Calvin, who in my reverie resembles the Misfit from "A Good Man Is Hard to Find."

"I guess I gotta take you to the hospital."

"You do, they'll send me back to prison."

I tell her they can't do that, but what do I know about criminal justice in north Mississippi?

"Jesus, please let him take me to Pontotoc. Please, Jesus, please."

As she prays and begs, I remain noncommittal but perhaps leave her with the impression I am taking her to Pontotoc, which happens to be in the same direction as Gentry, and maybe for the first ten miles or so I also think I am taking her to where she so desperately wants to go. But, no, as it turns out, I am not taking her to Pontotoc. Halfway between Grampus Lake and Gentry, I cross that line where kindness fails. A good man would drive her into the woods of Pontotoc and get shot by Mr. Calvin and his gang, but good men are hard to find and I am only one of Stella's jaded saints, most of whom are heavily armed. As soon as we hit Gentry, I veer off the highway into the ER entrance, and Pamela instantly starts weeping and begging *please, please, mister, you said you would, you promised, you promised you'd take me to Pontotoc.*

I park the cab in front of the ER's plate-glass window.

"I can't. I'm sorry. I'll get fired if I do."

That's a lie. Stella desperately needs drivers. I could probably disappear for a week and she'd hire me back.

"At least come inside with me. Please don't let them send me back to prison."

I sigh and tell her okay and go inside and explain the situation to the nurses, who promise me Pamela won't get sent back to prison. If they have to, they'll even let her spend the night on the couch. "But don't tell her we said that." I sidestep Pamela on my way outside and leave without saying goodbye. I feel bad about that, too, but it's been a long morning and I am hungry and tired. I slink back into my taxi and drive away feeling instantly better because Pamela is gone.

But of course she isn't gone. None of them are. They are always with me, all my meth heads, plus the guy sniffing his TV dinner, the long-faced farmer covered in grasshoppers, the hundred-year-old man in his hospital gown, the Goth girl, the howling baby, they are all crowded into the back seat of my Town Car like some demented team photo I glimpse, only for a moment, every time I check the rearview.

# CANCER MAX

I switch from Beethoven to Sam Cooke and haul a regular to work
at the Winchester plant, which makes a type of bullet. Next I haul
a waiter to Applebee's, which makes a type of food. After that, I pick
up my regular Leesha from her decrepit trailer park off Route 5.
While in my car Leesha is invariably talking on her cell to someone
who never says a word. Leesha manages at Burger King. When I
pull into the parking lot there, I wait for her to hang up and ask if
some kid named Orion applied for a job last week.

"He's about sixteen? Long face? Works at Popeyes?"

"Oh, yeah, I remember that boy. Quiet."

"Yeah, Orion's real quiet at first. Anyway he told me he applied. I've
been taking him to Popeyes for months. He's a good kid. Dedicated.
On time. I like him. Just saying."

"Okay, I'll look over his application."

Once she's gone, I park the cab and step outside to stretch. The
front bench seat won't adjust in any direction and plays hell on the

back spasms that ended my bartending career. After doing some stretches, I brush off the floor mats with their Crusade-cross logos and while doing this I discover an Adderall tablet crannied beside some green pill shaped like a tiny submarine. I pocket the green pill—I'll identify it online later—then down the Adderall with a swish of Red Bull backwash and grab my paperback and slide into the Boston Strangler.

The seat directly behind the driver is called the Boston Strangler because, while sitting there, any idiot can get you around the neck with his belt and demand your kitty before dumping your body among the broken speakers of some abandoned drive-in. Imagining my own murder—you are more likely to die violently as a taxi driver than with most any other job in America—I open my book and try to read, but the Adderall has yet to kick in and I can't concentrate enough to stop the letters from crawling around the page. It's so quiet with the engine off that the effect is cricket-like. If I listen hard enough I can always hear crickets.

The paperback I'm not reading is called *The Book of Eights* and it's about early Buddhism. I'm hoping the book might help me stop screaming at traffic. Bill Hicks called his inner demon Goat Boy, and my own version of that creature usually emerges around noon and takes over the wheel. Although I'm only on the third chapter, the book has already taught me that almost everything I thought I knew about the Buddha was wrong. As it turns out, the original Buddha, this cat Gotama, held no truck with God or gods and thought religious doctrines, gurus, ceremonies, debates, and metaphysical speculations all dangerous distractions. What we call the soul, Gotama compared to a river in constant flux, and he called all human contentions a "wilderness of opinions."

Wilderness of opinions. Well, Gotama has my number there. Actually I am a demolition derby of revved-up opinions crashing into each other. As the Adderall sparks my brain, I start lowering myself into the forests of ancient India until the Bluetooth rings in the forest, scaring the shit out of me, and it's Stella sending me on a rehab run.

"Oh no," I say in a voice meant to inspire pity.

"Relax, Lou. It's the good rehab, the one by the VD clinic."

"Oh. Thank God. The last time I went to the sketchy rehab my fare wrote me an IOU for thirty bucks. He told me he'd had to jump out a window to escape—they were holding him prisoner—and he promised he'd pay me as soon as he got his wallet back."

"Did you list that thirty on your log sheet?"

"Yes, I listed the thirty bucks on my damn log sheet. You got your share even though I got stiffed."

"Well, this guy seemed normal. For somebody leaving rehab."

I stash the paperback and drive toward the rehab on Route 5. The center is built on a tiered hillside above the parking lot. When I arrive, the stairs are lined with people, most of them wearing scrubs. There's this stocky guy in a pointy blue birthday hat, black sweatpants, and a white thermal shirt holding a pizza box and making his way down the stairway hugging people, shaking hands, lots of goodwill here. Two men carry the guy's luggage down the wooden stairs, and I pop the trunk and let them load up the three duct-taped suitcases. Then I check my chess app and castle to delay defeat.

My fare's still pumping hands and getting hugs. It's like they're sending him off to war. When he finally reaches my cab, he places his pizza in the back and sits up front. The smell of baked pepperoni takes over the car and starts my stomach rumbling. This guy—his name turns out to be Max—has curly brown hair above a man-child's face that would be handsome were it not pitted with thousands of tiny BB-like scars, a feast of chicken-pox wounds ecstatically scratched.

I ask him where to. Before answering, he takes off his birthday hat and studies it. It's blue and glittery and has a green poker chip glued to the front.

"The, um, what's it called . . . Rebel Motel? You know it?"

"I do," I say and off we go. "Been there once today already."

"Yeah? What's it like? I gotta stay there till the doc gives me the all clear."

I hesitate, then tell him, "It'll do in a pinch. You can walk to the square at least. Hey, what's with the pizza party?"

"Oh. Little celebration. Three months clean. Man, it's been decades since I've gone that long. I've been addicted to smack since I was thirteen."

"Thirteen? How old are you now?"

"Forty-fucking-two. But now—get this—they just told me I got cancer. Pancreatic cancer. The doctors aren't sure how bad it is yet— or at least that's what they're telling me. I gotta stay at that motel till the doctors are done with all the tests. Plus I can't smoke anymore."

"Jesus, man. I'm really sorry to hear that."

"Hey, shit happens, you know? It's funny, though, how I was so proud of being clean and then, boom, dick-smacked by cancer."

"I pick up a lot of people from rehabs, but I've never seen anyone get a pizza party before."

"I think they felt sorry for me. I'm kinda worried they might know something I don't. You know, about the cancer."

I can't think of anything to say to that. Finally I cough and mutter, "Usually, when I pick people up from rehab, they make me take them to the nearest liquor store."

A strange look comes over his face and I realize I've put an idea in his head.

"Really?" he says.

"Well, not always."

He points to the low-slung brick building catty-corner the DMV.

"You know what that is?"

"That? That's the VD clinic, man. Trust me, I take lots of people there."

"I had to go there last week. I had a breakout of something called HPV—I'd never even heard of that before. I kept telling the rehab nurse I ain't had sex in years, but it turns out you can carry that shit inside your blood forever and it don't come out till you're sick enough or stressed to hell. A few days after I learned about the cancer, I woke up and my dick looked like a prickly pear."

"Holy shit."

"Yeah. At first I thought it was the cancer got it."

"Oh man."

"So they sent me to that clinic and after waiting for five hours these three women spread me out on a metal table. Two of the nurses were real battleships but the third one was this young beautiful black girl—just knock-dead gorgeous—eighteen at the most—and they put on the ol' rubber gloves and take off my drawers and cover me in a paper sheet with a hole in it they fit my dick through, then, after they wheel over this giant magnifying glass, the girl takes out this tiny medicine dropper of hydrochloric acid and starts dripping a drop onto every one of those wart things up and down my schlong."

"Holy shit," I repeat.

I have this condition where I can imagine things a little too vividly.

"It took over an hour for her to get them all. It was like the other two nurses were just standing there inspecting the job the black chick was doing. Like she was taking an exam on my dick. And the whole time it was happening, man, it felt like I'd been alien-abducted or something." He makes a half gesture toward my flying-saucer air freshener. "But, hey, no complaints. The next day there was only these white bleach spots on me. Three days later I'm back to normal."

"Damn."

"Hey, is that Bigfoot?"

"Yeah. It's pine-scented."

"Huh. What flavor's the UFO one?"

"Wintergreen. I mean, supposedly. But it was kinda a rip-off. It didn't smell like anything. It's decorative, I guess."

He studies the flying saucer as if trying to conjure some memory long repressed.

"That black chick was so beautiful, man. She could have been a porn star. Every time I looked at her, I started worrying I was gonna get a hard-on. The acid burned like hell, too—pure S&M stuff—but at least I didn't get a boner, thank God. And I felt so sorry for her having to do that bullshit. Seriously, what kind of a life is that? I'd rather be a smackhead than a VD nurse staring at dicks through a magnifying glass all day. I mean, seriously, at least being a drug addict has its perks."

A Libra, I am still weighing those two opposite fates on my inner scales—smackhead or VD nurse?—when Max asks me about cheap restaurants near the motel.

"I'm on a budget, to say the least," he adds.

We're still discussing cheap food—something I know a lot about—when we pull into the courtyard of the motel and park in front of the islanded booth. The owner of the motel is never in the Plexiglas lobby. He's always repairing something or removing bodies or wringing out blood. Cancer Max pushes the buzzer on the office door while I scan the rooms—the different colored doors—for the cranky old Vietnamese owner. No wonder he's cranky, though. How many suicides can you mop up after before it takes its toll, right? The old guy yells at everybody. It makes him furious when you can't understand what he's saying. The more furious he gets, the more impossible he is to understand.

Meanwhile, remembering the meth-head twins, I glance at the red door to see if there's blood seeping out from under it or a hockey mask hung on the knob. Instead I spot Tie-Dye smoking a Lucky on the sidewalk while staring at the sky. I follow her line of vision to a cloud that's shaped like a tombstone. When I look back down, she's waving at me. I wave back even though I'm behind tinted glass.

"You got friends here, huh?" Max says while getting back into the car.

"Afraid so. Hey, you might have to wait a few minutes if the owner's cleaning a room, but he'll show up. He's never not here. It's like fifty bucks a night. Just pretend you understand everything the old guy says or he'll start yelling at you."

I get out and begin removing his luggage from the trunk—my Town Car must have the largest trunk in the history of the American sedan. Then I pile everything at the foot of the wooden staircase that leads to the booth. I hate to leave Max standing there among his luggage, but, as far as I can tell, that's my job, to help the needy and then abandon them as quickly as possible. He pays me with ten crumply ones, counting them out carefully from his hand into mine.

"Max," he says afterward, and we shake.

Right at that moment I catch sight of the owner shuffling toward us holding a small mop over his shoulder like a parade rifle. This guy is always walking into a squall. Every time he closes his eyes it's bloody beds. I avert my face as he approaches. I'm worried he'll recognize me from the few pre-Miko drunken liaisons I've had at his motel.

I'm about to escape—fares are waiting, after all—when it occurs to me that Max isn't strong enough to carry his luggage across the parking lot, so I wait for him to register and load his luggage back into my trunk and motor him the twenty yards to his room, the one with the sky-blue door, where I unload the luggage again and take it inside for him.

The room is clean enough but smells of slit wrists.

Before I leave, I tell him about EverSaved Ministries and suggest he call them up. "It's possible they'll help foot your motel bill. They do a lot of that type stuff." I explain how EverSaved is paying for two women to stay in that room over there, and I point across the courtyard—Tie-Dye is gone now—and say, "If you knock on that red door, they might be able to tell you more about it."

"Thanks. I'll do that. Are they pretty?"

"No, they're meth heads."

"Ever since I been clean I started thinking about women again."

"Yeah, well, good luck with that, but I'd be careful around those two. They're being stalked by some guy named Jason," I add before shaking his hand again.

On my way back to the cab, I notice a flyer has been taped to some of the doors. The flyer is advertising one of the art-hop things the local hipsters have here periodically, and it says that rooms 10 to 15 will be open to the public tonight and lists the local painters who will be displaying their works. There's also live music in the parking lot.

I climb into my cab and while backing out I glimpse a familiar face. It's Tony—he's standing outside the room with the faded yellow door, and he's about to light a cigarette when he spots my cab and quickly wheels around and goes inside.

Wait—*was that* Tony? I can't be sure. Is it possible that I've made a mistake—the same mistake I made last night when I saw him hitch-hiking on the highway? Maybe he's dead and I'm just seeing his ghost, I think in order to console myself. Then I remember that Stella asked me about Tony yesterday, and suddenly I know it has to be him. Still, it makes no sense. Last I heard, Tony was under house arrest in Kansas City, so there is no good scenario for him being holed up in the Rebel. Oh God. Not Tony. My heart plummets and I decide to repress the situation. After all, I've got dispatches to answer. Usually it's dead around lunch hour, but today I keep getting niggling calls coast-to-coast on the interstate. Meanwhile I'm starving. It's like I can still smell that pizza. I do two campus runs, then pick up an injured guy back at the Winchester plant and take him to the Urgent Care. His hand is wrapped inside a white towel, but he seems in an okay mood about it.

"You know there's a pizza back here?" he says as he gets out.

Sure enough, Cancer Max forgot his pizza. You might wonder then, do I take the pizza back to the motel? No, I do not. Instead of doing the decent thing, I sit there in the parking lot of the Urgent Care and wolf down a slice. Sorry dying-of-cancer guy, but that's my rule: anything left in my cab that isn't a cell phone or a wallet is a tip. Cell phones and wallets we have to take to the police station—at the end of our shift at the latest—everything else we keep. This is the tip you didn't give me, cancer dude, except you did, subconsciously, man, you tipped me this pizza for unloading your luggage twice after enduring that hideous story about genital warts that will haunt me forever.

I take another bite and chew it down. It's a cardboard-cold Pizza Hut thin-crust that tastes like grief.

# OSCAR THE AMOROUS OCTOPUS

This pizza, man. This pizza has done me no favors. Lying in the black coffin of the back seat, I lift my paperback off the Pizza Hut box set on my stomach and belch. The taurine-meets-Adderall effect has increased the cricket count in my brain a hundredfold—more crickets than a bait shop—and before long it feels as if I am suctioning the book's contents into my chirping brain. While reading I am surprised to learn that the path to Nirvana, as prescribed by the original Buddha, does not seem particularly virtuous in nature. The idea of compassion doesn't get much play here—something I find encouraging. In fact, the middle path this guy Gotama championed seems less like a religion and more like a twelve-step program you'd use to kick booze or junk. But in this case it's conceptual thinking you have to quit. The Buddha described the human mind as a sense organ, like a tongue or a nose, except the mind ravishes physical objects by layering them inside concepts until what you see in front of you is a mirage of sorts made up of opinion, need, prejudice, fear, and superstition.

It occurs to me, as I pause to release a fish stringer of burps into the cab, that Gotama appears to be arguing that traffic lights aren't really possessed by demons and that the only reason I keep flipping off red lights and curse-jabbering their mothers is because I am personifying and projecting religious beliefs onto mechanical objects incapable of malice. Although I remain skeptical about this theory, I keep reading, humoring the Buddha, until a text message bings in.

It says, "dont tell mom mn town".

Instantly I know I should tell Stella that her jailbird son Tony is in town, but I've a bellyful of bubbling acid and can't muster the energy to reenter Stella's whirlwind. Instead I pick up two construction workers who are helping to build the new hospital on Barbour Boulevard. One of them goes out of his way to call Obama that word four times before I drop them at the Super 8. Per usual, I keep my mouth shut when ferrying bigots. They all have guns, I assume, so I just clench the wheel and weep inwardly. At least I'm hitting the green lights now, which figures. Traffic-light demons love bigots. Every time I have a racist in tow it's a sea of green.

I'm still thinking about the Buddha, and how naïve he was, when I pick up this college kid from a barbershop and take him to Frat Row.

"Hey, don't I know you?" he asks.

I check the rearview. The local frat boys all look alike to me. They all have that swoop haircut, like hat hair but on purpose. In south Mississippi we were raised to hate these rich upstate kids, and I've never quite gotten over that hate. That's probably what the Buddha meant by concepts, too. I'm not seeing the actual kid in the back seat, I'm seeing the rich punks I grew up loathing.

"Didn't you used to teach here?" he asks.

Fuck. I consider lying but then fess up.

Yeah, I mumble. Kinda.

"You don't remember me?"

Reluctantly I glance into the rearview again.

"No—but I'll remember your essays if you tell me about them."

"I was in your Shakespeare course."

"That's the only one I ever taught. I got fired after that."

"You were always so nervous. Like you were about to run out of the room."

"Yeah. I was born that way."

I hope I'm not blushing. I hope Stella, who loves to tell our customers I am a retired professor, is not watching this particular episode of *As the Wheel Turns*.

I cough a few times then confess, "I'd always wanted to teach Shakespeare, you know? But then I sucked at it."

More dead air as the opportunity to contradict me passes.

"It's like you'd always forget the words. You know, like, halfway through your whatever speech."

"Soliloquy."

"Right, soliloquy, and you'd always forget right at the best part. Like you'd get going really good, then—"

"Yeah. Sorry, man. Sorry I fucked up Shakespeare for you in this life. But you should give him another chance."

"Dude, I'm never reading Shakespeare again as long as I live. The only reason I signed up for that class was the time slot. I didn't even know it was about Shakespeare until the first day."

I nod, don't comment. It wasn't even a real Shakespeare class, it was just a required freshman writing course that allowed the instructor to select a theme for the class, and the theme I picked was comparing

Shakespeare to hip-hop. I thought that would make it interesting. But then on the first day I found out every student in the class hated hip-hop. All they listened to was country.

"How's your son doing?" he says.

"My son? Good as new. Thanks for asking."

"That really sucked. After you came back to town—after his wreck, I mean—I didn't even recognize you. When you first walked in, I thought you were another substitute teacher."

"Yeah, I bet."

"Everybody felt sorry for you."

"Thanks, I guess."

"Were you on some kinda drug when you came back?"

Again I consider lying but instead tell him no.

"I was just hungover a lot."

"I heard you got fired for getting into a fight with a student. Like, you know, a fistfight."

"That's not true. I mean, it wasn't a student I got into a . . ." My sentence tails into a sigh. "I had a great Shakespeare teacher when I was your age. It changed my life. I wanted it to be like that for y'all. But then everything went . . ."

"The class was okay sometimes." To cover that lie, he asks, "Hey, is that Bigfoot?"

"Yeah. It is."

I drop the kid off on campus and drive to Walmart to get some petrol. I'm talking to myself out loud while pumping gas. People are noticing but I can't stop. Wow, I really didn't need that.

It was in the middle of my only semester teaching that my son got hit by a drunk driver and went through the windshield. When I got the call they told me to bring a funeral suit. I spent the next three weeks sleeping in the ICU waiting room with half a semester's worth of Shakespeare soliloquies spin-cycling my brain. The doctors had no idea if Kevin would wake up. We didn't even know if we wanted him to live. He had so many tubes sticking out of him, so many casts and bruises and incisions, it was killing me to stand over his bed, but the big worry, according to the doctors, was that his brain had been severed, that the corpus callosum, the nerve center that joins the brain's two hemispheres, had been torn. I couldn't stop talking to myself inside my nest of pillows in the waiting room. I guess I really never stopped talking to myself after that. Some internal dialogue got the upper hand and a type of Tourette's took over in which I couldn't quit cursing at inappropriate moments. I would sit in my corner of the waiting room and bargain and curse and mutter until I noticed somebody looking at me and I'd try to stop but ten minutes later I'd be back at it. I couldn't stop flipping off ghosts. Finally I'd have to sit on my hands.

Kevin, who was twenty-two then, eventually emerged from his coma angry as hell, a different kid from the one I loved. Certain lobes awoke while others remained dark. The doctors said we'd have to wait for the swelling to go down before we knew anything, but at least his brain hadn't been severed. He had always been a cautious, sweet kid by nature—bright-smiled and hyper-polite—but the lobes that woke up first created an id child who only wanted to escape the hospital or hit on the nurses. At times it was like we were dealing with my son's smarmy twin, Opposite Kev.

Mostly what he wanted to do was walk. Within days of regaining consciousness he started ranging out into the hospital halls with me following him pushing his IV stand. He behaved like a drunk frat boy. Even his voice sounded different. It wasn't my son, yet somehow it was. I'd trail after him for hours late at night through the dark corridors. The hospital felt like a gloomy maze. It felt like the afterlife. We walked so much I started getting back spasms and had to lie down on the floor of the corridors while Kev glowered over me waiting impatiently for me to get back up so he could continue walking.

Then one morning everything changed. How it happened was I bought him a large cup of coffee from a nearby bakery—he'd been refusing to drink the dank hospital brew. His long-term memory lobes hadn't woken up yet, and the doctor had instructed me to show him familiar objects to see if he might recognize them. So that morning while we drank our coffee I held up the wallet he'd given me on Father's Day. It had the Football Club Barcelona coat of arms on it.

"You recognize this?" I asked.

He studied the wallet a moment, then grinned and said, "Yeah. I was going to get you the wallet that said *Bad Motherfucker*, but Mom wouldn't let me."

By the time he'd finished his coffee he was whole again and we kept chatting away about Tarantino movies all morning. It was almost scary how quickly he turned back into himself. If you've ever seen a skyscraper light up at dusk, that's what it felt like. One floor of lights came on, then another, all the way to the top.

I'm still talking to myself while cleaning my windshield at the pumps. While exiting the station I spot my colleague Cecil parked in the Walmart lot and pull up beside him. Cecil is early seventies but looks younger. He's a Sioux Native American who fought in 'Nam and suffers from post-traumatic stress, and yet he is by far the most laid-back saint in Stella's crew. There is something childlike about Cecil. He just wants to be left alone to watch lesbian pornography in his cab and pick up fares in peace. He's very polite, almost demure. We have an alliance in this game of taxi survival.

But today Cecil's got his dander up, having had a hospital run himself. Cecil hates hospital runs. He's convinced we don't get paid for them at all. I disagree. I think we kind of get paid for them if we're stubborn. But neither of us is sure. Stella preys on our shabby memories.

"Even when she pays you she doesn't pay you," Cecil sulks.

"Exactly. Stella's superpower is she doesn't care if you catch her ripping you off. It's all water under the bridge to her. She doesn't hold grudges and doesn't think you should either. My ex-wife was the same way. We'd have these vicious arguments, and then an hour later she'd be like, 'What?—you're still mad about that?'"

He considers that a moment, then points out, "Stella doesn't hold grudges unless you go to work for another cab company. Then she hates you forever."

Cecil is wearing his Vietnam vet truckers cap as usual. I'm pretty sure that cap must help tremendously with tips.

"She can't afford to hold grudges," I say. "Hey, guess what?—this sucks but I'm pretty sure I just saw Tony at the Rebel Motel. I hope I'm wrong. But I'm pretty sure it was goddamn Tony."

"Oh no. I thought he was under house arrest in Kansas City."

"Me too. Did you ever hear exactly what it was Tony did?"

"No. Which is strange. It must have been bad."

"I heard it was just drug dealing."

"No, I think it was worse than that."

I pause in case Cecil wants to elaborate. My sense is that everybody knows more about it than me but that nobody's talking.

"You think I should tell Stella?" I ask.

"I'd stay out of it."

"Good. I was hoping you'd say that."

"Actually maybe you better tell her."

"Fuck."

Cecil is about to take off for the afternoon. Due to his age, he is one of the rare drivers who doesn't work dangerously long hours. As soon as he's gone, I'll get swamped with calls. While we are parked window-to-window, Cecil shows me an old black-and-white Polaroid of his family and starts telling me who everybody in the photo is and how they died and what they did and why he loved them. Cecil is the most earnest person I've ever met. I have to be careful when talking to him because he takes things so literally. He's our most sane driver and maybe our least sane, too. For instance, lately he's been forgetting to turn off the porn when picking up fares. Customers have been complaining to me about it. One of them was a ninety-year-old woman.

Before leaving, I give Cecil the leftover pizza. He seems pretty psyched about that, which is another thing I like about Cecil: he is easily solaced. When I tell him I'm late for Anna, he grins and looks away. The joke here is that I get saddled with all the blue-hairs because I'm the only one with a car low enough for them to climb inside. Anna is my most regular regular—she's also the one who complained about Cecil's porn. The other drivers all call her my girlfriend. This is hilarious to them because Anna is extremely small and a little hunched over with a lovely intelligent face and a strikingly white bouffant hairdo that must be tended to at the Ashley Fly Salon once a week. Because of her new titanium hip she has to go to Gentry Rehab three days a week for physical therapy. She has loads of children and grandchildren, but it's me who takes her everywhere, including the liquor store for her weekly handle of Old Charter. I don't charge her for the liquor runs because I know she doesn't want her children—they foot the taxi bill—to see that on her account. She tips me the difference. Anna's cool.

I've never met her kids, but I certainly don't like them. They should take their mother to church. They should take her to the grocery store. Anna is so small she has to ask strangers to hand her canned goods off the high shelves. She is not steady on her feet. One day I had to pick her up off her living room floor. She was more mortified than hurt. I carried her to the back seat and took her to the ER.

Today she's not ready when I arrive at her tiny apartment so I wait outside and write Stella a text that says, "Think i saw tony at reb motel?? not sure was him. mighta been a chimp smoking a cig."

I erase the last part and send the text.

By now I'm worried Anna's dead. This happens every time she's late. I'm terrified I'll be the one to find her body. But she's not dead, just running late. I hold the door and buckle her in, which is an awkward type of physical intimacy. After today's cavalcade of meth heads, being with Anna feels like entering a Zen rock garden. She's so soft-spoken I have to concentrate like a demon to discern what she is saying in the deep back seat. She has that aristocratic Southern accent that wealthy people in the north of the state have cultivated. (It's my people in south Mississippi who have that imbecilic syrupy accent.) Usually Anna and I talk about books, religion, or the upcoming election. Anna's a Methodist but strives to be open-minded while following a doctrine that discourages that. She's a Clinton Democrat and a voracious reader, although her taste leans toward C. S. Lewis. After she learned I'd once published a book—Stella told her—I had to beg Anna not to buy my novel at the local bookstore.

"Please don't, Anna," I told her. "I'm a really dirty writer. I'm not apologizing—the world needs dirty writers—but I don't think C. S. Lewis would enjoy my book."

The novel I had published some twenty years earlier is remembered locally, if at all, for a chapter in which the main character, a seventeen-year-old kid, fucks a watermelon. Therefore the literary question I get queried with most frequently is, "Hey, aren't you the guy wrote that book about the kid who fucks watermelons?" Here again we see the relationship between obscenity and memory.

I was horrified Anna would actually read the damn thing and begged her not to, but she did, on the sly, and claimed to love it. "It's so unfair you're driving a cab," she said. "If I were rich I'd be your patron." Yeah, Anna's cool. She has great dignity and loves Jesus. And I can see in her eyes that she's distressed about me being a Buddhist, but, being a Clinton Democrat, she knows better than to broach the subject of my inevitable writhing. It worries her, though. She once asked if she could pray for me, and I said sure, Anna, have at it.

"They doing your acupuncture today?" I ask once we're on the interstate.

"It's not acupuncture, Lou, and you know that. It's dry-needle therapy. And, yes, I'm getting it again today. I'm quite excited about it."

"It's acupuncture, Anna."

"How do you know? Have you ever had acupuncture?"

"Yeah, I did. Back when I lived in Vermont, I had this cold-weather-induced asthma. So I'd go in to this acupuncture guy and he'd strip me down and cover me with needles, like I was a porcupine, then he'd leave me spread out on the table that way all alone for like half an hour, and I'd just lie there feeling weird. He even stuck needles into my face, all along my sinuses, and he'd always put one on the tip of my nose that I couldn't stop staring at."

"Did it help your asthma?"

"It did, I think, but I couldn't keep doing it. I have this needle phobia and it was like living out some kind of demonically reoccurring needle dream. He'd put needles into my feet, into my eyebrows. Then he'd twist the needles to activate the chi energy. And every time he twisted one it felt like getting zapped with electricity."

"That's exactly what they do in dry-needle therapy."

"See, I told you it was just acupuncture with a fancy name."

"Oh. I almost forgot. I have that book to return you. Thank you for lending it to me. I finished it last night."

"Did you like it?"

"I did, but it took forever to actually get to the world's fair."

"Yeah, that's like the most wholesome book I've ever loved. If somebody had described the plot to me I'd never have read it. It's like a time capsule of wholesomeness."

"It was exceptionally wholesome. Except for, well, that part about the octopus molesting those women."

"Oh, yeah. What was his name?"

"Oscar. Oscar the Amorous Octopus."

"Right. Oscar. That was my favorite part of the book. Actually that might be my favorite passage in literature. Doctorow's the best dirty writer there is because he sets you up with wholesomeness, then— boom—hits you below the belt with the dirtiest scene ever, and it's always pure-poetry dirty, and funny. I mean, I'm sorry, I know it's wrong, but I was laughing like hell while that octopus molested those women."

"Do you think that really happened? Could that have been a historical part of the world's fair?"

"You mean do I think there was really a tent at the world's fair featuring a perverted octopus named Oscar and a bunch of beautiful women swimmers who got molested by Oscar every hour in front of hundreds of fairgoers? Is that what you're asking me, Anna?"

"I suppose it is, Lou."

"Funny you should ask me that, because it just so happens I did a little research, and it turns out there's no official record of the perverted octopus tent at the 1939 World's Fair, but apparently Doctorow got that story from an oral history done at the time—from some guy who claimed to have worked in the octopus tent. Not only that, the guy claimed it was his job to manipulate the mechanical octopus to undress the swimmers."

"I couldn't believe what I was reading. I was just so astonished. But it was beautifully rendered."

"It was. He's the best dirty writer ever, a god. I guess I should have warned you."

"Well, I'm glad I read it. And anyway I think you enjoy giving me dirty books."

"I probably do. It's always fun to try and shock Methodists."

I park in the handicap slot at Gentry Rehab, get out, undo her seat belt, help her outside, then walk her to the front door and open it for her. I'll have to reverse-order all of this in an hour. Horace is dispatching now and keeps me running solo through rush hour while he sucks pig. First he sends me way out on Route 40 to this regular named Liston who lives in a trailer off a dirt road and claims to be running for mayor of Gentry. He's a black Republican who used to drive a city bus until he got fired. Stella once tried to hire him for All Saints, but the city wouldn't approve his license.

"Bad politics," she told me.

Liston's a short muscular guy about fifty with a roundish freckled face. The last time I gave him a ride he was headed to the Toyota dealership intent on a new Camry. He said that a politician needed to make a good impression.

"The party's real interested in me these days and I need to look sharp."

That ride was supposed to have been his last in my cab. On our way to the dealership I asked him how he could run for mayor when he didn't live in the city limits.

"I wrote down my sister's address."

I nodded in a kind of "ah" way. I wanted to ask how you could run for mayor if you don't have a job but decided not to. Liston's answers tended toward diatribes against the black community. He was always being harassed by other black people because of his politics. He's even been beaten up a few times.

There was this other Republican black guy in Gentry who used to stand beneath the Confederate soldier statue on the town square and hold up the rebel flag to traffic. He was pro-flag and used to get beat up so often that eventually the cops stationed an officer to stand guard near him. His name was Clem and for many years he was Gentry's most devoted activist. Clem ended up meeting a black woman at some Tea Party gathering who was also into the rebel flag—there's somebody for everyone—and they became a couple until one night, driving home from a rally, the two of them became convinced somebody was following their truck. Clem called the police—911 recorded the whole incident—then he sped up, lost control of his pickup, ran off a bridge into the Tallahatchie River, and the two of them drowned together in that river without anybody ever writing them a song.

That day I took Liston to the dealership, I thought he was gone forever, but now he's back. I pick him up at his trailer and pop the trunk so he can throw his duffel into the maw. Sometimes Liston has a bunch of stops before the laundromat, and I'm hoping that's not the case today because I need to pick up Anna soon and new dispatches keep pinging in.

"I thought you were leaving me for a Toyota," I tell him.

"Toyota turned me down for the loan."

"Yeah. Those fuckers turned me down, too. I wanted to get my own car. That way you get 90 percent of the drop instead of 50."

"Why'd they turn you down?"

"Well, to start—they had lots of reasons—because I'm not an employee. I'm an independent contractor. Even though I've paid off a mortgage, I'm not even eligible for consideration for a loan."

I pause and then ask why he got turned down.

"Too many hospital bills from getting beat up," he replies. "I'm pretty sure they'd turn down Jesus, too."

"Yeah, probably. Carpenters are independent contractors too."

The pizza I ate is still tormenting my stomach. Speaking over my gut, we begin a rambling conversation about the unfairness of life. We're both mad at the world by the time I drop Liston at the laundromat. Plus I'm hitting nothing but red lights now. They are definitely haunted and it's definitely a fucking conspiracy. Part of the problem here is that I give a damn. You simply cannot care this much about being on time while driving a cab. If you do, your heart will go through the windshield. But, at the same time, I can't stand to think about Anna standing there clutching her purse outside the rehab center worrying about me. Whenever I'm late, she always convinces herself I've had a wreck. Anna and I spend a lot of time worrying that each other are dead.

When I hit a fresh red on Barbour and Lott, the second-most evil traffic light in town, it happens. I can feel it like a werewolf sniffing moonlight. My nails begin to grow and I fiddle with my collar and mutter, "Jesus, it's hot in here," as the goat horns slowly emerge from my skull.

# NEVER BLINK YOUR HEADLIGHTS AT A UFO AND OTHER DRIVING TIPS FOR MISSISSIPPIANS

Your main job as a driver in Mississippi is to anticipate stupidity: the door flung open into traffic, the Doberman leaping off the truck bed into your convertible. Constantly paste the worst-case scenario over the road ahead of you and never stop asking yourself the question: "What is the stupidest thing that idiot can do right now to get me killed?"

Or try this method. Pretend you are Trinity and that the world outside your windshield is a Matrix program in which any driver can transform, like that, into Agent Smith mere moments before attempting to savage you with his automobile. Never for a moment forget that everyone is trying to murder you. Most of them aren't very good at it. Others are very good at it.

Or just assume that everyone is masturbating furiously.

Every moment spent in reverse can ruin your life. Crank your head over your "other right" shoulder, place your hand behind the seat back for leverage, take your foot off the brake, and assume the worst. Do not go one inch farther than necessary while reversing.

Safe driving is all about the neck. Pride yourself on how much you employ your neck while changing lanes. Approach driving as a neck exercise.

Never purchase a pickup truck that isn't at least four times as large as you need it to be. Obviously if you do drive a somewhat smaller truck, a friend of yours, or maybe somebody you'll never meet, might insinuate behind your back that you are gay or have a small dick, or God forbid, both.

Get rich, become an asshole, raise obnoxious children, then buy a huge motherfucking SUV twice the size of God so you and your precious goddamn litter get to survive the wreck that mangles and kills the poor family in the human-sized car you just decimated while texting.

Sunglasses look ironic on a corpse. They also make brake lights difficult to see. And sunglass frames invariably create a blind spot when you are looking over your shoulder to change lanes. In most situations sun visors work fine.

Never use the turn signals on your monster truck because if you do all the people behind you in traffic will instantly assume you are impotent.

Before merging onto the highway from an on-ramp, look over your shoulder to make sure the near lane is open, then, while merging, glance from your side-view mirror to your rearview mirror to double-check that no car has appeared behind you. Using both mirrors eliminates blind spots. But only use the mirrors after first cranking your neck.

Nothing good ever came from making eye contact with an idiot.

Never block another car's ability to swerve into the fast lane while it's passing an interstate on-ramp. Never blind-spot follow any car—seriously, don't!—but especially don't blind-spot follow in the fast lane when passing on-ramps. You will get sideswiped, and it will be your own damn fault.

Never forget all those times you started to change lanes and got your dumb ass honked at by the innocent woman whose family you almost murdered with your laziness. Use your neck. You are lucky to even be alive.

Never blink your headlights at a UFO unless you want to be seriously fucked with.

Don't drift onto an exit ramp (or into any turn). Get off the road fast. The lunatic without insurance behind you—see him there?—hey, that's me!—he has mistimed your drift and is about to clip you from behind and send you spinning. Don't drift, goddamnit, cut the wheel and turn.

Try using cruise control in the city. It reduces stress by allowing you to concentrate fully on the road and not have to glance at the speedometer and search for speed traps. Also, it makes it easier to spot UFOs camouflaging themselves inside cumulus clouds. Cruise control makes for a professionally smooth ride.

Don't tailgate the guy who is refusing to tailgate the guy who is going criminally slow. There is a special ring in hell for people who do this. By the way, if you have ever done this to me, then I've got two points for you to consider.

In road rage situations, when somebody starts following you, drive to a police station. Lock your doors and keep moving. Running a red light is better than getting beaten with a tire iron. Stay in the right lane so you can take a right on red to avoid giving the incel psycho-killer behind you adequate time to turn off his Ayn Rand podcast, get out of his car, and start exploding your back windshield with a 12-gauge.

Don't tap your brakes when somebody starts tailgating you. It's tempting, but it can backfire. Also don't flip him off, not yet. First try this: pretend to adjust your rearview, so that the asshole knows he has your attention. Then suddenly wave to him and smile as if you are excited to see him. This will make him worry that he knows you, and instantly he will feel like the dick he is and fall back sheepishly. Then flip him off.

Whenever you see a cop immediately start picking your nose. Likewise, once pulled over, grab a tissue and blame everything on the flu while blowing your nose in as disgusting a manner as possible. Cops are similar to human beings in that they want to get away from people with colds. Also, most sneeze-induced infractions are not considered reckless driving. If you have to murder somebody—just saying—the I-was-sneezing defense might get you off with only a few years served.

Though largely unsatisfying, there are alternative gestures to the middle finger. The ironic thumbs-up works okay, as does the "meh" gesture of waggling your palm. I also enjoy trotting out the index finger circling the temple to imply *you are fucking insane, you assclown moron!* Or just freak them out by pretending to be using eloquently obscene sign language. These gestures will not get you killed. But every middle finger is a roll of the die . . .

Let it go. They all have guns and minuscule dicks and secretly want to die.

No matter how fast you drive, you don't get there any sooner. This maxim, though blatantly false, was one of the first pieces of advice given to me as a cabbie. What's a few minutes on either end? Sometimes on an interstate I'll set the cruise control to 2 mph below the speed limit, turn on some good music, and let the world pass me by like tubing down a river.

You can judge a driver by her windshield. This was one of the first pieces of wisdom ever given to me by Stella. Think you're a good driver? Go look at your windshield, brother. That's how good of a driver you are.

Weirdly, having a dick doesn't make you an awesome driver. I thought I was a fantastic driver until I started driving a cab full time and almost killed dozens of innocent people. The first step to becoming a good driver is to admit you are a bad driver.

Get a clamp to holster your damn cell phone. Jesus God, don't ever drive holding a phone in your hand. Hate everyone who does without ceasing.

Don't take selfies at red lights. It makes you look like a superfreak and is so dispiriting for others to behold it shatters their view of God and humanity and makes them desire an alien invasion.

Stop layering concepts such as prejudices and superstitions over the objects and people encountered while driving. There is a part of your great-ape DNA left over from hunting and gathering that wants to prejudice all things into tribal categories and layer them with attributes. No race or gender is a better or worse driver. They are all horrible-horrible drivers with their eyes glued to goddamn cell phones googling new ways to kill you.

When driving on a college campus assume everybody to be sleepwalking from Ambien overdoses. I once stopped my cab mid-traffic and watched a student studying his phone march directly into my grille.

Don't pass cars on the interstate while using cruise control. Get the hell out of that car's blind spot fast and pass while still accelerating. And don't veer back into the slow lane too quickly just because the dickwad behind you is riding your ass.

Rotaries are known as *roundabouts* here. This is where you are most likely to be T-boned and sideswiped at the same time. In Mississippi you must exercise patience while the driver ahead of you studies the rotary, discarding various theories and adopting others, before lurching forward against the flow of traffic. Avoid at all costs using the rotary's two-lane system to pass another car. That is what fucked up Dante. The person in the lane beside you is always in the wrong lane at the last second and will swerve into your door, and there you go.

Never fuck with anybody in a Dodge Charger. They are all Mississippian Satanists, which is the great white shark of Satanists.

Never vote for any politician who reads books about city management and road systems because if you vote for a politician who reads books somebody might, behind your back, insinuate that maybe you are homosexual. In fact, all decisions in life, especially what presidential-candidate bumper sticker you put on your car, should be based entirely on what better promotes your heterosexual prowess.

Every time you hit a particularly evil red light immediately remind yourself what both Bill Hicks and the Buddha taught: life is a dream that exists inside a flash of lightning. It's all a dream: your beater car, the empty bank account, the cheating wife, the neighbor's dog barking incessantly all night, you, me, that cop with the speed gun, the socialist fucking your daughter, this, that, the other. Reminding yourself the world is a dream is a natural form of detachment that instantly helps ease road rage, plus it will give you lucid dreams at night where you can go flying around the cosmos like a flying saucer and have astral sex with dead celebrities.

# KILL TEDDY! KILL TEDDY NOW!

*The world confuses me. Why is the first guy at the light always the last to see the light change to green? Can somebody explain that? Are there any physicists here tonight can possibly explain this fucking phenomenon to me? Wouldn't you think speed of light distance, the first guy would be, I don't know, the first to see the fucking light change? Wrong. It's always the last guy, who has to go through nineteen other cars. Go, go, go, go, go, go, go, GO!—it's green!—that's as green as it gets—I'm gettin' older—GO! Finally this guy snaps and putters through the yellow. Oh shit. I'm stuck at the same fucking light, and I'm thinking, "I hope that guy dies on the way home. I hope he's cut in two by a train in front of his kids. They can watch both halves of their moron daddy wriggle like worms on a hot pavement. You're too stupid to fucking drive. You shoulda been a blow job. Fucking idiot." Then, behind me, I hear, "GO!"*

Road rage, as Bill Hicks knew, is always there, slumbering beneath the skin, ready to break through the eggshell of your belly and devour the Sigourney Weaver of your sanity. The bane of cabbies, road rage can kill you firsthand or second-, the heart attack or the exit wound.

At this stage of the day I am best imagined as a demonic goat wearing knockoff aviators behind tinted glass. I am driving around flipping off my fellow citizens for committing driving infractions I am guilty of every hour. I'm bleating at red lights and gurgling at pedestrians while tailgating an old lady with my hooves pounding the wheel, my teeth grinding, my body bent forward, my horned head ratcheting in circles.

It's early afternoon with Horace sending me every shithouse dispatch and drunk-drugged Stella camped in my Bluetooth giving me contradictory dispatches and unwanted advice. The problem with Stella is that she really misses driving. She knows her routes by heart and loves to show this off by crawling into my ear and backseat driving me around town. Stella quit driving because of something that happened to her in the projects one night. She told me about that terrible thing on the day I met her. In fact she told me about it in grisly detail during the first twenty minutes of a job interview in which I sat there aghastly wondering if she were drunk or crazy or if this were perhaps some ingenious job-interview technique. She kept telling me more awful details— things I can't repeat—things I should not have been hearing— things I should not presently know.

Before I can fetch Anna from dry-needle therapy, Stella orders me to pick up another regular, this guy Teddy. Normally I would double up when it gets this busy, but in this case the two passengers are incompatible. Teddy is a pathetic drunk who lives in a condominium suburb east of town in which, I shit you not, all the streets are named after Confederate generals. I pull into Stonewall Cove and park. Even though I'm trying my best to be an atheist today, I'm praying Teddy doesn't have Tiffany, his insidious gold-digging girlfriend, in tow. If you had to say something nice about Teddy, you might, following a long pause, mumble something like, "Well, compared to his girl-friend, Teddy's endearingly grotesque."

Yes, being a human freak show, Teddy is at least entertaining, and he's also generous when blackout drunk, which is always. Tiffany, a late-thirties fallen Tri-Delt, is desperately trying to get Teddy to marry her because he's rich—he's Mr. Hundred Dollar Bill and tips a C-note most every round-trip ride yet I am the only driver on staff who will still pick him up. That's how horrible a person Teddy is (yet Tiffany is far, far worse). Teddy's saving grace is that he is 95 percent incoherent, his words a stream of slurred nonsense with the occa-sional syllable of recognizable English peppered in. Often those moments of coherence contain words like *pickaninny* or *negro.*

When I pick them up, Teddy and Tiffany are dressed in their Stepford finest and she's helping his drunken ass falter in the direc-tion of the Town Car. You'd think they were crossing a raging river rock by rock. I'm behind the wheel trying to gauge whether Teddy's drunkenness warrants my assistance. While getting into my cab he's fallen down on numerous occasions. He's also set my floorboard on fire with a dropped cigarette and left a giant burn mark there that Stella is going to murder me over once she notices it. I sigh and get out to help spill Teddy into the front seat while Tiffany takes the Boston Strangler.

Teddy calls Tiffany "Tiff." Here's all you need to know about Tiff. The two of them used to be engaged years ago, but then Tiff left town with another rich guy, which caused Teddy to deteriorate to the point that he was institutionalized and stopped drinking for two years and became a human being until Tiff ran out of gold-digging money in Atlanta and returned to town.

"And Teddy fell off the wagon my first day back!"

She's told me that gloriously romantic story at least nine times. It's a great source of pride to her. Whenever she tells it, Teddy grins in confirmation and adds, "Bena'drunkin'evadasin."

Sometimes when Teddy's passed out in the cab, Tiff will come over the back seat and start suckerfishing my neck. On other days Tiff will climb into my cab alone and get me to pick up her other boyfriend, Drunk Jim, who happens to be Teddy's only friend in the world. Later, when I pick them up from whatever bar they've infested, Tiff and Drunk Jim start fooling around in my cab. I'm not a peeper but more than once there's been a distinct funk. Every time they do this, they put the fare on Teddy's account and stiff me. Once they left a used condom on the floorboard.

Today I am taking Teddy and Tiff to Miguel's, the Mexican joint near Walmart, but first we have two stops to make. The first stop is a liquor store for tomorrow's breakfast. The second stop is to pick up Teddy's father, the former state senator, and his doddering wife. Per always, Tiff and Ted are in the middle of a drunken brawl when they slosh into my cab. Actually *brawl* implies a two-way street. With them, it's just Tiff railing upon and physically hitting Teddy, who is just conscious enough to grunt, moan, and grin in reply to the abuse. Before we can even turn off Nathan Bedford Forrest Boulevard, Tiff is already hitting him, ponging Teddy's head back and forth from the back seat, while calling him every name imaginable—real venom here—and trying to make me corroborate her theories.

"Have you ever seen a bigger loser of a drunk fuck in your life, Lou?"

Teddy flop-tilts his head in my direction to see how I will respond.

"Teddy's okay," I reply. "Teddy's a prince among men."

Teddy grins and fumbles with his wallet a few minutes before spilling a hundred-dollar bill onto my floorboard. I scoop it up and place it in the plastic cup I use for a tip jar and say thanks, man.

Because Teddy is from an important family, Stella values him greatly as a customer and usually calls me when I have him in the car to remind me to be polite. Sure enough, the phone rings while we're stopped at the liquor store.

"You're positive it was Tony you saw at the motel?" Stella asks me.

"I'm pretty sure, yeah. But why would Tony be in Gentry?"

"I got no idea. What's going on with Teddy?"

"He's in the liquor store."

"Alone? You let him go in alone?"

"He's not as drunk as usual," I lie.

Most days I go into the store for Teddy, but today I was in a cruel mood and enjoyed watching him tack nose-first into the glass door.

"How long's he been in there?" Stella demands to know.

"Like ten minutes? I've been trying to call Anna but she's not picking up. Goddamnit keep your hands off me! Sorry—I was talking to Tiffany. And will you please tell Horace to get off his ass and take some ten-dollar runs. Oh shit. A cop just pulled up."

"Get Teddy out of there!"

I hesitate. The truth is that a part of me wants Teddy to get arrested. After all, I've already scored today's C-note. And if he gets thrown in jail now, I won't have to pick him up from Miguel's later.

"Go get him!" Stella screams.

"Okay, okay, I'm going."

I stroll into the store and sure enough the cop is interrogating Teddy, who appears to be made of quivering jello. I tell the cop I'll

take care of him, sir. "I promise, I'll get him home." Then I inform
the cop that I am a cabdriver, as if that somehow recommends me.
The cop squints in my direction and asks to see my taxi license.

"Okay he's your responsibility," the cop decides. "I got your name
writ down."

"Butahdudbuymalikkeryet," Teddy says.

The cop looks at me until I shrug.

"Let's get you to the car, Teddy. I'll come back for your breakfast."

I buy three bottles of J&B before we go fetch the senator. I don't
know what to make of the senator. I mean, he's a bad drunk, too, but
he's at least coherent. I guess I don't understand his tolerance. If
Teddy were my son I'd beat him to death with a bag of hammers. But
the senator seems resigned to Teddy.

When we get to the senator's house nobody is home. It turns out
there's been a misconfiguration and the senator and his wife have
already driven to the restaurant in their BMW. While Tiff is figuring
this out on her cell, I am watching a dark stain grow across the lap of
Teddy's khakis. I don't otherwise react to this stain, though I suppose
on some level I am recalling the Buddha and what he said about
observing people without attraction or aversion. I'm thinking that if
the Buddha had met Teddy and Tiff he might have retired from the
forest to become a bounty hunter. I can feel the Tourette's or whatever
it is wrong with my brain steaming my blood into a fine red mist. I
just want to be left alone to scream into the void. My inner Goat Man
grabs me by the throat and snarls, "KILL TEDDY! KILL TEDDY
NOW!"

Instead of killing Teddy, as I probably should, I pull him out of my
car and mop up the seat with paper towels while the two of them go
inside to freshen up. Ten minutes later they reemerge with Teddy

wearing a pair of the senator's high-water khakis. It's a new day and we're off. When I drop them at Miguel's, Teddy tries to tip me another C-note, but I'm so pissed off I won't even take it.

Stella calls me again, and I interrupt her barrage of madness to inform her that I'm going to get Anna now.

"Anna can wait," she snaps. "Go get this guy Stanton back at Walmart. His family owns a bunch of prisons. Make a good impression."

Prisons? Wait—families own prisons?

"Go-get-Stanton!" she yells when I try to explain how long Anna has been waiting.

I almost mutiny, but in the end I abandon Anna.

"Me cago en tu puta madre!" I scream at the next red light. That's right. "I shit on your bitch of a red light mother!" Excuse my Spanish y'all, but, being a Barça soccer fan, I have a repertoire of curse words guaranteed to get you red-carded at Camp Nou. "Que te folle un pez!" I scream at an elderly pedestrian. "I hope you get fucked by a fish, you son of a whore!" After a pause for breath, I add, "Vete a freír espárragos!" although it's not clear to me why *go fry asparagus* is considered such a terrible insult in Spain.

Outside Walmart I get my demons under chain long enough to call Anna. Did she forget her phone again? I'm parked by the pharmacy entrance and am trying to compose myself. After all, Stella wants me to impress this rich guy . . . what was his name, Stanton? I do some breathing exercises but can't stop cursing. Part of the problem is that I can still smell Teddy's urine emanating from the leather. I grab the Ozium, spray some near my face, and inhale it. Then I try to follow my breath, to relax more with each exhalation. This works okay until I catch sight of this mid-thirties white guy shoulder-strutting toward my car, the preppie frat boy grown up and wistfully contemplating the prisons he will inherit.

"Oh no—not that Stanton," I mutter.

Please, God, give me any other Stanton.

The Stanton I am watching exit Walmart is this rich punk I once got into a fistfight with late one night at the bar of the Oasis Diner. That fight happened at the end of a bad year that started with my son's coma and ended with me crashing my Vespa and shattering my clavicle. After two months on my couch riding the opium pony—I had a catheter stuck into my stitches that allowed blood to drip into a plastic bladder-ball I had to carry around with me—I finally healed enough to venture outside one evening. And that was the night I got into the fight with Stanton, who is currently walking toward my cab but can't see me through the tinted glass.

He is not going to be impressed. No, he is not going to be impressed at all.

That night at the Oasis, I'd been sitting on a barstool beside my friend Kyla, a tall, imposingly beautiful woman with long blonde hair who'd fled to north Mississippi after losing everything during Katrina. Her husband, Earl the golf hustler, was seated on her far side from me next to Vance, who owns the diner. We were there to hear our friend Jean Paul's punk-country band that prides itself on changing its name every gig, and I was enjoying myself but arguably mixing opioids and tequila to an unenviable degree when this guy Stanton strutted over—he didn't know me from Adam—and draped his body across my injured shoulder like we were old war buddies, then, instantly forgetting I existed, he began screaming into my left ear toward somebody at the right side of the bar, at which point I politely told the motherfucker to get his goddamn arm off my shoulder. He retreated to his barstool but was too drunk to remember my warning, much less my face.

The fight that ensued was entirely the fault of Kyla, who, as soon as Stanton retreated, began telling me all this damning gossip about him. She wasn't trying to get me to fight him, it's just Kyla's nature to comment on folly. She hates rich idiots.

"If I were a man, I'd punch guys like him in the face every day," she said. "Trust me, I have a list of guys I'd punch."

Kyla was still telling me what a reprehensible person Stanton was when he suddenly reappeared and once again draped his arm around my stitched-up wing, causing me to experience a series of pop-pop-pop pangs along my screws and sutures. Once again he started using my ear as a megaphone. This time I shoved him off me and cursed him roundly until he slunk back to his barstool, which might have been the end of it had not, at that moment, his equally drunk girl-friend decided to get involved and slur-warn me that I'd better be careful because I didn't want Stanton coming over here to kick my skinny ass.

To which I very unBuddhistically replied, "Yeah? Hey, here's how worried I am about that. HEY STANTON!"

I kept screaming his name until I gained his attention and then began flipping him off with both hands fluttering around my face like mating butterflies. "Fuck you!" I kept mouthing. Then I turned to his girlfriend, smiled, and yelled over the band, "That's how wor-ried I am about your boy."

Stanton came off his barstool after me. A lot younger than me, stock-ier too, but also a lot drunker and shorter, this prep-school creep could easily have lost a fight to a game rabbit. I was feeling confident—yeah, I'm liking my odds here—until it occurred to me that I couldn't hit him with my right arm because of the stitchwork. And, like many men who should never be in bar fights, I own no left. My left arm is that kid you knew in kindergarten who broke his nose playing tetherball. I have no left and if I throw my right then God knows what kind of pain will soar through my cosmos. Meanwhile here comes Stanton ready to rumble, baby. Me, I got no left, I got no right.

Clearly I should have thought this through—it's all Kyla's fault!—but finally, at the last moment, just as he's raising his fist, I devised a plan. The only athletic activity I've ever been really good at is heading a soccer ball. There is something Zen-like about heading a soccer ball. Also heading a soccer ball gets you high. Maybe that's why I'm good at it. I tend to excel at things that get you high. So, for the first time in my life—here comes Stanton!—I decided to transform the art of the Zen Buddhist header into an act of despicable, concussive violence.

And, wow, it worked really well! Did you see that? Damn, son. I wish I'd known about the Zen head-butt thing back in high school.

After head-butting Stanton, I looked into his blue eyes. He was still standing, but that was only because the ceiling fans were turned off. The baseball cap he always wore had come off to reveal a bald dome, which aged him and made him resemble a chemo patient. At this point I could have pushed him over with one finger. Instead I hit him with a stunted right cross that hurt me more than it did him, and he staggered backward obligingly, a drunk falling off a boat, and collapsed cruciform onto the dance floor, causing Jean Paul to strike the wrong chord on his punk version of "Seasons in the Sun."

Jean Paul and I stared at each other a moment, then I looked down at Stanton—he was bleeding from the cheek and motionless. Suddenly aware that everyone in the crowded bar was staring at me, I began massaging my shoulder in Jim Rockford manner and walked back to my drink and picked it up with a shaky hand and told Kyla, "That was so your fault."

What I will only reluctantly admit now is how good head-butting Stanton felt. It had been a hard year in which I'd probably prayed and cursed more than I had my whole life combined. Aside from my son coming out of his coma, punching Stanton was the highlight of that year. And I started feeling even better about the fight when it became clear that the person I'd knocked down was the most despised preppie in town. Everybody kept slapping me on the back, which really hurt. Tom the bartender slid me a free drink. Only Vance thought to wander over and check on Stanton. The band hadn't stopped playing, although nobody was slam-dancing any-more. Vance helped Stanton to his feet and they went outside to talk. Instead of worrying if I'd be fired from my new job teaching at the university, I sat there at the bar basking in my pathetic glory, and it was a beautiful thing. Until I got fired from my new job teaching at the university.

And now, years of misery later, here's this guy Stanton—the guy I knocked out cold—walking toward my cab. This is what they call karma, right? God. Karma. Is it the same thing? Is karma like a mil-lion evil Shakespeares forever re-revising the soap-opera plotlines of our lives? Is that what you're thinking? I'm with you. That's what I'm thinking too.

Please, please use the back seat. At least give me that, God—or karma or whoever you are doing this to me.

Stanton opens the front door and gets inside.

"Hey man," he says casually, and it occurs to me I might be off the hook here. Maybe he was so drunk that night he won't recognize me. Nevertheless as I drive with Stanton beside me I am radiating awkwardness. I've tried not to be proud of that fight even though as bum rushes go it ranks alongside losing my virginity. No wonder so many people beat me up in high school. It feels really good to beat up the weak. Yet now it does not feel good one bit because this guy Stanton seems humble and shy. He's not humble and shy—he's just one of those jerks with no sober personality—a void who drinks to achieve identity. I know plenty of guys like that. They are shrinking violets until they are assholes. I'm stealing glances at Stanton during right turns. He's wearing a sky-blue baseball cap above brand-new jeans and a short-sleeve plaid shirt, the overall effect being comically wholesome. Does he recognize me? If so, is he afraid? Or is he plotting revenge? Is he about to shoot me with his pocket pistol or stab me with his trusty barlow? Stranger things have happened in cabs.

We travel ten minutes in silence until I pull into the apartments where just yesterday—was it yesterday?—I picked up Zeke the Unabomber. Choctaw Ridge is such a squalid complex that at least two different drivers from All Saints live here. The parking lot is filled with broken teeth, and the dumpsters are overflowing with garbage and crows. Stanton, rich boy that he is, is obviously here to score drugs. Before getting out of my cab, he turns to me and says, "Do you know who I am?"

You can ask that question many ways. He's asking it in a curious yet slightly belligerent manner. Maybe he thinks I was so drunk I don't remember the fight.

"Yeah. I know who you are."

I say this with minimum malice, as if bored. I'm hoping this doesn't get ugly. I just want him gone. I just want to fetch Anna home.

After a pause he says, "You sucker punched me."

I stare at a mockingbird hopping around the lid of an aluminum garbage can.

"No," I tell him. "I head-butted you. After telling you three times to sit down. You were swinging at me, man."

"Head butt? Really?"

He seems honestly surprised.

I nod. I'm pretty confident he has no memory of this because that's what he told Vance after the fight. "What happened?" he'd asked. The guy had just woken up on the dance floor with no idea how he got there.

"I got fired from teaching because of that fight," I tell him.

Stanton nods digestively and makes his decision and sticks out his hand. "No hard feelings," he says uncertainly. We shake. When he tries to pay me, I tell him I got it, man. I don't apologize, which is what I should do. Instead I give this rich jerk the free ride I didn't give the destitute Goth chick.

After Stanton exits my cab, the sun appears between clouds and suddenly I'm aware of the dust swirling in the air all around me. The dust seems alive, sentient, like those tiny sea monkeys I once flushed down the toilet as a kid. In the advertisements they wore little crowns and smiled jauntily. In real life they were hard to love. While remembering that swirl of sea monkeys, I'm staring between dumpsters to where some guy is throwing a baseball to a kid, and suddenly I realize it's Zeke playing catch with his daughter. I close my eyes and— remembering all the evil thoughts I've harbored against Zeke— recalling what an asshole I was to head-butt Stanton—I take in a deep breath filled with sea monkeys and then howl them through the windshield.

# FREAKHOLE

As a young man I once read a book from which I have never recovered. I don't know if I'm glad I finished reading *The Naked Ape* or not, but it was a profound argument that demonstrated just how close we as a species still abide to the trees. Once I got to the chapter about how, as with other monkeys, our genitals have been replicated onto our faces to ensure we never for a moment stop thinking about reproducing, I knew, a part of me did, that if I kept reading this book there was no turning back. Therefore, at the tender age of eighteen, while I was a student at Pearl River Junior College in Poplarville, Mississippi, the author Desmond Morris convinced me that human beings are best understood as only relatively great apes—let's face it, the chimps and bonobos are not bringing much to the table—and that once we accept this bitter pill called zoology then suddenly all our treacherous and seemingly illogical behavior makes perfect sense. The only thing *The Naked Ape* didn't explain to me was Shakespeare, who was probably a space alien.

My sea-monkey scream triggers a bowel movement situation, so I have to stiff-leg it into a nearby Wendy's, where, mid-dump, Stella calls and orders me to go pick up Stanton at Choctaw Ridge. She says it's an emergency and hangs up before I can argue. Unable to scream at Stella, I start haranguing whatever ghosts abide inside bathroom stalls at Wendy's until somebody knocks on the door and asks if I'm okay in there. A few minutes later I slink into my cab and flip off Wendy as I drive away.

It occurs to me that you might be asking yourself by now what exactly is wrong with this boy? Meaning me—and yeah, I get it, a valid question. You haven't seen me at my best, but, okay, I concede some psychoanalyzing might be in order. Here's my theory, for what it's worth. There is something called the executive function of the great-ape brain, which is our dopamine-based communication CIA headquarters that keeps us sane and gibed. A series of maladies circle this headquarters like buzzards, and they have names like ADHD, Tourette's, OCD, bipolar disorder, post-traumatic stress disorder, paranoid schizophrenia, etc. etc. etc. (etc.), but, thing is, if you're on record as having one of these afflictions, you do not have it in a pure form but instead have it mixed with symptoms from the other buzzard maladies. In my case I suspect an eight ball of ADHD and OCD laced with Tourette's and a pinch of schizophrenia. Not the end of the world, you're thinking? Yes, there must be something that can be done to help me, but, hey, I'm an independent contractor in Freakhole, Mississippi, and therefore have no access to any mental-health resources whatsoever, so fuck me I can't even see a shrink much less get put on some magic pill. No, all I can do is flail in traffic sputtering obscenities as you, blithely riding your designer antidepressants, steal my right-of-way while texting your agent about your latest book deal.

Where is my prescription, friend? Buddy, can you spare one of those second-novel pills? Just drop it on the floorboard and I'll find it.

When I return to Choctaw Ridge, which I also flip off, nobody emerges from inside an apartment. I'm so tired that I try hitting the horn that doesn't work. I don't have a phone number for Stanton, and I'm not sure which door he went inside, but I suspect it's the one I'm currently flipping off with the Harley parked out front. That would make sense because that's the door I least want to knock on. To make matters worse, I've got that Billie Joe McAllister song stuck in my head like I do almost every time I do a pickup at Choctaw Ridge.

I walk to the door with the hog out front. I already know what I'll find inside. We've all been inside that efficiency apartment with the cabinet doors that aren't flush and the dun-colored carpet with the fake wood paneling in the living room and roach-themed wallpaper in the kitchen. I'm half expecting to find all the ghosts from my back seat huddled on the couch passing a bong.

The door opens.

It's Moondog!—or I think it is, but he's got a different look to him that throws me off. Also he's holding a paintbrush—not a big one like for painting walls but a dainty one like for painting landscapes. This seems very weird to me. I mean—then—wait—huh?—I notice an easel behind him supporting an actual painting, and it's a watercolor of a taxicab, an old blue Continental with suicide doors. There's an old photograph of the same car taped to the top of the easel. In his watercolor—maybe I'm dreaming this?—maybe I'm about to wake up and start my day driving all over?—the long blue sedan is parked on the town square in the taxi slot facing the Oasis, and the whole painting is, well, *it's pretty.*

"Moondog?" I say and glance away from the painting long enough to note Stanton dead on the purple couch. He looks peaceful in death, almost saintly, a fallen icon. His hands are folded over his chest, and a beatific smile lingers on his face. Then I do a quick pan around the room to discover every wall is crowded with paintings of the various taxicabs that Moondog has driven at one time or another—dozens of them. I recognize some of these cars, especially the Lincoln six-door with a floral decal spanning its back window that says DISCO LIMO. In Moondog's painting you can see the disco ball hanging from the ceiling inside the cab, and the interior is filled with speckled light thrown by that ball. It's done in acrylics, I think—I don't know much about paintings—and the limo is parked in front of Syd's Bar and you can see people you know— people I recognize—inside the bar.

That goddamn Tallahatchie Bridge song, the verse about *pass the biscuits please*, is getting really loud in my head, and I want to buy at least three of Moondog's paintings on the spot except I'm too taken aback to even think that clearly. I mean, shit, Moondog's a biker. When we shared a cab—he drove it nights, I drove it days—he was a scary dude who practically throttled me when I asked him to please clean up after his shift because he'd returned the Town Car with blood smeared all over the back seat. Back then I thought of Moondog as a beast, a druggy biker, but fuck me he's a goddamn talented artist.

I really need to get this song out of my head, man.

"Lou!" Moondog says, like he's greatly relieved to see me. "Good, good. Come in, come in, man. Long time, brother, long time. Looks like you got to take freakboy here home. He's kacked, man, utterly kacked."

The apartment smells like wet dog, and there's so much fur on the purple velvet couch it's like a beagle has exploded. As I step inside, a door bursts open in the back and two little kids run shrieking through the room chasing each other around a coffee table that has a large handgun centered on it before disappearing into the other back bedroom. Following those kids, my eyes settle on a pressboard bookshelf filled with a dozen or so books, hundreds of CDs, and a grinning collection of those kitschy Mexican demon skulls with horns.

"Don't ever have children," Moondog tells me.

"What'd you do to Stanton?"

"What'd I do to him? Goddamnit, what's he doing to me?—the idiot swore this wouldn't happen again. Look, we're gonna have to lug him out to your cab. Hey, you still driving my hot-rod Lincoln? I fucking love that car."

After saying this, he points to a canvas leaning against an air-conditioner vent. The painting—I think it's done in oil maybe?—is of the Town Car, but painted in better days when it had Crusade-cross rims, and it appears freshly waxed as it motors past the record store and the windows of the cab reflect the buildings it's passing and the painting is kind of perfect, and I want it, want it bad, except there's a price tag of $250 stuck on its brown plastic frame.

"That's fantastic," I blurt.

"Yeah, I'm trying to finish all this up before the art thingamajig tonight. You know, at the Rebel? I paid for a room but the painter I was splitting it with backed out two hours ago—motherfucker—so now I got to sell like two paintings just to break even—good luck with that, right? Also I gotta come up with a name for my collection—that's one of their rules, like every room has to have a sign outside it advertising the art inside." He goes to the window and pulls back the curtain like he's worried about cops. "Hey, you'll never guess who I saw yesterday standing on the side of Route 5?"

"Tony. So where do you want me to take this freak?"

I study Stanton to see if he'll react to this barb, but he remains motionless, his hands crossed over his chest. All he needs is a coffin. And maybe a wooden stake sticking out of his heart. Suddenly I'm imagining a vampire painting of Stanton on the couch. Suddenly I'm an artist, too.

"It was Tony! Fucking Tony! You believe that?"

"Is Stanton even alive, man?"

"At first I wasn't sure it was Tony standing there, but an hour later he starts calling me, dig? Starts calling me! Him calling me! Again and again."

"What'd he want?"

"Fuck if I know. Like I'm answering that asshole? Screw that guy, but he must be on the lam—I mean, he was wanted for attempted murder."

"Attempted murder? I thought it was just a drug deal thing."

"It was. Until Tony attempted to murder the drug dealer."

The goddamn Tallahatchie Bridge song is finally almost over. God, I hope it doesn't start up again. Poor Billie Joe. Killing himself over and over again every time this song gets played on a jukebox. He's probably committed suicide more than anybody else in history, more than my dad even.

Suddenly I realize why Moondog looks so different.

"Holy shit—dude, you got hair," I say.

"Yeah, plugs. Hurt like hell, too. Like taking a nail gun to your head—boom-boom-boom."

He mimes firing a nail gun into his head—or I think that's what he's doing. He seems kind of speeded up to the point of panic. The song in my head starts playing again from the start. Billie Joe, he's got to jump off that bridge one more time. Or maybe he was pushed, man. Maybe he was pushed.

"You like the look?" Moondog asks me.

"I do. Wow. You could star in a Western now. You look just like the Marlboro Man."

And he does. At least from the neck up. His angular face is suddenly movie-star chiseled. He's not wearing a shirt, just frayed cutoff jeans that are way too short for such thin, long thighs. The body beneath his head appears extremely spindly, and his posture is terrible from decades of driving cabs. The effect is mid-renovation, as if the head has been completed and the body will be replaced next.

"The last taxi driver," I tell him. He looks at me confused until I explain. "You know, the name, for the art hop, the sign, by the door? You're like the last real taxi driver in Gentry, right? Uber's coming to town, we'll probably all be homeless beggars soon, and you're like, I dunno . . . like, the last . . . never mind."

"No, no, I get it, I like it. Hey, grab his legs, okay?"

"I can fucking walk!" Stanton suddenly wails into space from his prone position without otherwise moving in any way.

We both jump back from the couch. That was quite unexpected.

"Hey, that's my novel," I say, pointing to the bookshelf.

"Yeah. Man, I really dug that scene where all the high-school kids show up at the landing pad to watch the medics unload Lynyrd Skynyrd's body parts."

It's the first time anybody has mentioned that scene to me, and I am about to hug Moondog when he asks, "Dude, you really fuck a watermelon?"

I lower my arms and stare at the grinning skulls lining the top of the bookshelf. The demon skulls are all different colors: red, yellow, green, blue, and black. I gaze into the eye sockets of the black one as I answer him.

"Nah. I bought a watermelon to, you know, maybe like research fucking it. I kept telling myself I should fuck it. I kept saying, 'Faulkner would fuck that watermelon.' But I never did. Biggest mistake of my life. I'd probably be famous now if I had."

"I heard you got in a fight with Stanton there."

I suck in one side of my cheek and stare at the couch.

"I heard you sucker punched him."

"You should paint him. He looks like vampire Jesus."

"He looks like a fucking corpse of himself is what he looks like. We gotta get him outa here before my old lady gets home and starts shooting up the place. She told me that, told me she was gonna shoot us all dead if I ever dealt out of the house again. You believe that shit? What kind of mother shoots her own kids, right? Jesus."

I ask where I'm supposed to take Stanton.

"Take him home, dawg. Take him home. You know that."

"Yeah, but where's home at?"

"Ah, good question." Moondog picks up his cell, as if to investigate, then puts it down and decides, "Let's get him into your car first."

"No way. I want that address first. Hey, you still driving for Rock Away?"

He starts searching through his phone again.

"Yeah. It's great. Like we use a radio to dispatch. I don't know if you've noticed, but everybody at All Saints is fucking insane. I can't believe I drove for that crazy wench fourteen fucking years, man. It's a miracle we didn't murder each other. A miracle."

"What if he doesn't wake up by the time I get him home?"

"I'm fucking awake right now!" Stanton yells, his head rising off the couch for just a moment before he dies again.

It happens so quick I'm left wondering if I imagined it.

"Just prop him up against the mailbox. It's 2012 Country Club Road."

"Shit, okay. 2-0-1-2. Let's go. I'm late to pick up Anna."

"Anna? I fucking love Anna. She's my honey."

"Yeah, she's cool."

"Best blow job I ever got."

"Man, fuck you. Don't talk about Anna that way. She's old."

"It's my house, dawg. My house."

I study Moondog's handgun a moment. I don't know much about guns but it's the kind with the spin cylinder thing and the hammer you pull back like in Westerns.

"Yeah, well, why don't you just keep Stanton here in your fucking house, and I'll go pick up Anna, who's like a hundred years old and doesn't need you talking shit on her."

"Relax, man, relax. I'm just jokin' you. How's Anna doing?"

"She's got a new hip, man. She fell down in her kitchen because her goddamn kids put in cheap linoleum tiles. I'm the one found her there and took her to the ER. Maybe I should take this asshole to the ER, too, huh?"

"I'm fucking fine!"

"See, he's fucking fine, he's stellar, no prob. Look, do me a favor and don't put my address on your logbook, okay? And don't tell nobody you were here today."

Right as he says that, there's a knock on the door. It's the loudest knock I've ever heard. Three sledgehammer blows, then silence. The song in my head comes to a halt so quickly I can hear the needle scratch.

"Holy shit," I say.

Moondog scurries to the window and spies out again.

"Fuuuuck," he whispers like a tire leaking air.

He makes a strange face at me. It's the kind of face you might find on someone hanging from a rope. When he makes this face, I suddenly see the plugholes beneath the budding turf of brown hair. His eyes are really large and really green, and his bird-wing moustache connects to his sideburns. He's like six-and-a-half-feet tall but must weigh in at a buck twenty. Which is odd, because I remember him being much stockier when we shared the cab. Is he dying of something? Would a dying man get hair plugs? And that face. It's uncanny. I can almost see him playing poker in a saloon. It's the face that sold a million cigarettes yet he has the arms of an eighty-year-old man.

When the pounding starts again, Moondog places an issue of *High Times* over the handgun and opens the door, and it's like opening a kid's picture book to an illustration of a giant with a tall bleach-blond Mohawk. This particular giant is wearing an open leather vest with no shirt beneath it. The shark from the *Jaws* movie poster is tattooed across his belly.

"Jase, what gives?" Moondog says.

It's obvious Moondog is trying to block the giant from coming inside. The giant also has something wrong with his face that might be horrible acne. It's like there're polyps of running wax pooled in teardrop columns along his cheeks. The eyes planted inside this ravaged face are arctic blue.

Suddenly, and without a word, the giant thrusts his hand forward. He's holding a small piece of paper in that hand as well as a notepad and pen. Moondog appears to be familiar with this behavior. He carefully takes the paper and reads it. Then he says, "I'll get my tools. Let me see the cash first."

The giant stares him down until Moondog decides he doesn't need to see the cash after all and disappears into one of the bedrooms. I'm alone with Jase now. Why does that name sound familiar? I'm sure I've never seen him before—he'd be impossible to forget. His arms are covered with liquidy tattoos, a barrier reef filled with tentacles and jellyfish and moray eels. His body is ripped, and the various bulges make the sea creatures appear to be undulating.

Jase strides inside, glowers down at Stanton, fishes out his wallet, removes a handful of bills and cards, and then drops the wallet onto the floor. He turns around and notices me watching him.

At that moment, from the back of the apartment, Moondog yells, "Jason, this is Lou. Lou rides a Vespa."

Jason stares at me like he's trying to set me on fire with his eyes. It makes me remember when I was a kid and used to ignite bugs with a magnifying glass.

"I really liked that movie," I tell him. "It made me want to be a marine biologist."

I've barely finished saying that when his blue eyes switch gears and grip me like a tractor beam. It feels like I'm being pulled into him. Like he's sucking my soul into his blue eyes.

"Jase don't talk," Moondog announces while coming back into the room holding his toolbox. "It's some kind of religious doodah thing, right, man?"

At that moment, still trapped inside his gaze, I suddenly remember Glossolalia Jason, the guy who got set on fire by the meth-head twins, and this realization hits me so hard I actually cover my mouth with one hand and try to back away, but I can't—his tractor beam has me.

While still staring at me, Jason rips off a second sheet of notebook paper and hands it to Moondog. He must have had it written out in advance.

Moondog reads the note and says, "EverSaved? Yeah, I know them. Lou, they still have an account with Stella?"

I stumble over my words and end up nodding a lot. Meanwhile Jason is still transporting my soul into the ice chasm where the bodies are kept. My words, too. It feels like the words I'm trying to speak keep getting siphoned out of my brain into his blue eyes. I can hear Moondog's voice, but only vaguely, like a TV playing through a wall.

"EverSaved?" he says. "Yeah, they used to run that crazy women's shelter in Memphis. Somebody told me they shot porno movies in there."

"They just closed that shelter," I blurt. But, since my atoms are being dispersed into Jason's alien eyes, the words come out garbled, and I have to say them again like somebody learning English.

"They-moved-that-clinic-to-Tupelo," I add.

It couldn't be more obvious I am lying, but luckily for me Moondog is panicked to get us outside. When the two of them start to leave together, I ask, more loudly than intended, "Hey what about Stanton?"

"I'm fucking fine," Stanton screams into the air.

And, with that, he rises like Lazarus and walks out of the apartment and stands by the cab waiting for me. I'm the last one out. I glance back into the room, as if to say *let's go, ghosts*. There's a small roach on the spine of my novel. I'm tempted to mention something about the wisdom of leaving kids alone with a gun but instead decide to keep my mouth shut and walk outside into the monstrous heat. Moondog and Jason are standing by a windowless van that appears to have been spray-painted silver. Its side door is open, revealing a large motorcycle inside. I watch them for a moment as they start trying to remove the motorcycle from the van. By the time I slide behind the wheel of the Town Car, Stanton is already in the Boston Strangler and the girl in the song is dropping flowers into the muddy waters of the Tallahatchie River.

# MISSISSIPPI!

As I drive toward Country Club Road, I'm half expecting Stanton to come over the seat back and start stabbing my neck with a syringe. He has said nothing the entire ride, and I can't even see him in the rearview. It's freaking me out a little. He's just a lurking presence back there, a breathingness. We're turning into his suburb, which borders a golf course, when I realize he has no money. Does he even know he got robbed? Fuck! I check the address and pull into the driveway of a house that could sleep fifty people, all the lights off, no cars in the massive driveway, and Stanton gets out without a word and walks in front of the hood and up the many stairs into the dark empty mansion to quiver in ecstasy for hours or weeks.

I sit there doing the middle finger thing for a few minutes. Then, to calm myself down, I briefly consider burgling him. Finally, when it feels safe to drive again, I back down the long driveway and, while bottoming out, remind myself I need to swing by the Rebel Motel to warn the meth-head twins about Jason. But first I need to fetch Anna.

Twelve minutes later I have her in the cab. It's early rush hour and I'm backed up four rides when Anna asks can we please stop by the bookstore. *Et tu, Anna?* I close my eyes for the briefest shudder before saying *sure* and aiming us downtown for what will be at least a twenty-minute detour. As I drive, I'm trying to text Horace to pick up my fares, but the autocorrect keeps changing the message into nonsense. A lot of people seem to be honking at me, but I can't flip them off because of Anna. To my great shock there is a parking space open in front of Corner Books. I pull in and step into the godless heat and unbuckle Anna and hold open the doors of her life before walking into the air-conditioned bookstore behind her. It's my favorite bookstore in the world, but today its charms are lost on me as I slink among the hardbacks sneering at author photos and muttering *schoolteacher, schoolteacher, schoolteacher . . .*

I'm flipping off the author photographs—the MFA parade, man, they open those things faster than Starbucks—and muttering among the stacks of new books when—what's this?—I spot a coffee table book called *Mississippians!* The book is filled with glossy photographs of our state's most outstanding living citizens and even has a chapter on Mississippi writers.

*Hey, maybe I'm in here* a part of me thinks in spite of the fact I know damn well I'm not in there. Dirty writers, man, we're nothing to flaunt. Nevertheless I open the book to the section called "Mississippi Writers!" Not that I'm expecting to find myself, but, hey, you never know with this writing bluff, right? For instance, decades ago, shortly after I published my one perverted novel, I won this fellowship where I got to live in Tokyo for half a year with an expense account and my own apartment simply because I'd submitted a short story to the fellowship's judges about a twelve-year-old boy in

Mississippi who liked to climb pine trees naked and then jerk off to photographs of Yukio Mishima. Before flying to Japan, I had to fill out a questionnaire about what aspects of Japanese culture I wanted to explore. I wrote down, "Sex dolls!" Once in Tokyo, I was ushered by my two handlers through every assembly line of that poignant industry—I watched their eyes being put into their heads—and one afternoon I was even tour-guided through a Ginza showroom in which dozens of sex dolls, each of them worth ten thousand dollars or more, had been situated into a still-life bar scene. The dolls, dressed demurely, were sitting at tables holding faux cocktails or standing up along the bar—even the waitresses and bartenders were sex dolls. I walked among them turning circles of awe. You could almost hear the conversations.

So, yeah, you never know, I'm thinking as I turn the pages hoping to spot my mug among the *Mississippians!* Nope, nope, nope, fuck, fuck, fuck. Wait a minute. What the hell is Brady doing in there? He's from New Orleans. And Ann Marie, she's from Minnesota. And Stanley? And Kit? What the fuck's going on here? None of these Mississippi writers are from Mississippi. They're all MFA imports. It's a fucking conspiracy, man.

I'm curse-turning pages now. Customers are noticing. Eventually I notice them noticing and make myself put down the book and exit the store to wait outside in the heat, where I continue to murmur a kite-tail of cuss words at a nearby meter maid while staring across the street at the statue of the Confederate soldier. The movement of the clouds makes the statue appear to be falling forward. I flip it off and then make myself lower my hand and then grab my crotch and flip off the statue again. I can't stop doing this. I feel like a porno-graphic batting coach. Finally I get back inside the car to deal with my issues. Thank God for tinted glass or they'd have thrown away my key by now.

In need of music therapy, I blast David Banner's album *Mississippi* in an attempt not to lose my mind. While listening to the CD, which I do whenever I find myself teetering, I hold my fingertips to my temples as if trying to piece together a broken vase long enough for the glue to dry.

*We from a place (where dem boys still pimpin' them hoes)*
*We from a place (Cadillacs still ridin' on Vogues)*
*We from a place (where my soul still don't feel free)*
*Where a flag means more than me (in Mississippi)*

"You know what makes you a real Mississippian?" I rant or maybe just scream inwardly while flipping off the Confederate statue trapped in my rearview. "Surviving a Mississippi public education, that's what makes you a goddamn Mississippian. Nobody who went to some seg-ed prep school counts. In fact, if you got any kind of education before you turned eighteen then, sorry, you're disqualified. If you don't have giant gaps in geography—entire countries you're unaware of, major religions you don't know exist—then nope, not a Mississippian. If you had sober teachers who could even spell the word *matriculate* then you're from someplace fancy like Alabama. If you can multiply by nines or carry over numbers in long division or diagram sentences or know what the fuck that periodic table thing is all about or if you can make any sense at all out of *Absalom, Absalom!* then you're from someplace not Mississippi. Never learned to roll joints during racist bomb threats? Never watched cops disarm your classmates? Never crawled into your bed at night terrified that

Pascagoula UFO robot aliens with crab-claw arms and anal-probe fingers were spying in your windows? Then odds are you didn't grow up fiftieth out of fifty, so humpback-humpback this you are not a Mississippian!"

I'm still flipping off the rearview and ranting when I spot Anna trying to open the car door by herself—oh shit!—so I snap off the crunk and get her buckled in while blushing fiercely. I don't even ask her what books she bought, which I know hurts her feelings, but the last thing I want to do is expose my Goat Man voice to Anna. She can always tell when I'm stressed out, which in turn stresses her out. She knows that if I quit my job, her life will become miserable. The other hackies all frighten her—plus they have to lift her up by the armpits into their giant SUVs. In many ways I am Anna's outlet to the world. Understanding this, she tips me ten bucks when I drop her off. I take her house key and let her inside, at which point I know she is standing on the far side of the door praying for me. I stand there a moment with my head resting against the door absorbing her prayers.

Then, as soon as I'm back in my cab, I put on David Banner again and go full-court Tourette's behind the tinted glass, screaming, flipping off ghosts and gods, pounding the wheel, my head spinning in circles. While trilling out, I glance at my Shakespeare air freshener. "Hey, you want to be a Mississippian?" I scream at him over Lil Jon. "I can arrange that. I know people. I can make that happen."

Then, once the CD has worked its magic—I think it calms me down because it's even angrier than me—I pick up Liston at the laundromat and take him back to his dirt-road trailer.

"You okay, man?" he says as soon as he gets into the car.

"Don't ask," I reply.

I've switched to Al Green so as not to offend Liston's Republican sensibilities.

"You lookin' a little berated today." Liston studies me a moment longer and adds, "It ain't easy is it, brother?"

I glance over at him. At that moment tears blur my eyes. My theory is that every human being has a human being cowering inside them.

"No, it's not," I agree.

We kind of nod at each other. Yeah, it's always heartening when crazy people bond like this. We'll probably end up in neighboring padded cells.

After he gets out, I put on Mose Allison, who guides me through the next four trips without incident. Then I stop to buy another Red Bull. Have you been keeping count? It's way too many, but nevertheless halfway through what I think to be my fourth can I achieve an unexpected Zen state. So, yeah, keep that in mind, it's the fourth one that puts you over the top. Or was it my fifth? Either way, I'm feeling so good that when I hit the four-lane I set the cruise control to 58 mph and crawl into the back seat to don my spangled racist-state-flag wingsuit before climbing out the sunroof and balancing myself atop the Town Car like a redneck surfer with the traffic zooming down Highway 9 and then—you have to time this part perfectly—I leap into the wind and start gliding over Mississippi like a red-tailed hawk climbing thermals until I'm soaring high above the green ocean of scraggly pine. Look—there's the brown snake of the Mississippi. And that gleaming skyline is Jackson, our lovely capital and the place in America where you are most likely to be hideously murdered. And over there, near the putrid gulf, that's Hattiesburg, my hometown. Let's dive in for a closer look (flutter-flutter-flutter) and slalom down for a landing between all these steeples and religious billboards.

Look—over there!—that's the soft-porn drive-in where the owner supposedly kept both his dead parents displayed in glass coffins. And that's the regular drive-in, where the screen was actually a house the owners lived inside and where I once got to third base during *The Omen*. That's Hardy Street, our main drag. And Nick's Ice House, the plywood palace with toilet-seat barstools where I learned to shoot pool. There's the house I grew up in on Mandalay Drive. And there— Pasquale's Pizza!—I worked there nine years starting at a buck twenty an hour when I was thirteen. And that building complex there—see it?—on the far side of the tracks?—that's the first black school I ever got bussed to. Boy did I get my ass kicked there. And down here somewhere—hold on, let's zoom in closer (flutter-flutter-flutter) yeah, that's the gymnasium where I once saw this kid Stevie Halcomb, the only other white kid in sixth-period gym, getting raped by my friend Ricky Sylvester . . .

Okay, let's try for a landing in the student smoking section. God, I must have dipped a hundred cans of Skoal here . . . hold on! . . . here we go . . . pull . . . chute . . . NOW, man! . . . and . . . drift . . . down . . . down . . . coming in . . . getting close now . . . let's not Skynyrd this . . . oh shit, man! . . . wait!—what the?— BADDOOM-POW- WHAMEEE . . . FUUUUUUUUUCK! . . . CRASH-BOOM-BANG, MAN! . . . ow! . . . shit! . . . crap! . . . damnit!

Here we are, man. Real Mississippi! We made it. Let's clean the blood out of our eyes and have a look around. My old school, good ol' Lillie Burney, where I got knocked unconscious five times and almost died by various forms of torture nineteen other times. Memory lane, man. Let's try this door. No, no—wait, here's an open one. Wow, it's all flooding back to me now. Here's where I got my mouth busted open by that girl who slam-dunked my head while I was drinking at this water fountain. So much blood, man, so much blood. And here, this is where Brent Spencer once held me up against the wall by my neck—my feet off the floor—until I passed out and had this really cool dream about snow. And that's our principal's office over there. Good ol' Mrs. Bonaparte, who still gives me freaking nightmares. This way, I think. Look, my old homeroom! Let's creak the door open and peek inside. There—that's me, man!—on my first day of ninth grade—yeah, that skeletally thin kid with the dark circles under his eyes and the giant Adam's apple beneath that mop of brown hair staring up in horror at the American flag as we recite the Pledge of Allegiance. Look at how my hand is shaking over my heart. I am so afraid, man, because for the last five years I've been hearing hand-me-down horror stories, like something told around a campfire, about all the terrible things large black guys do to small white kids at Burney, and now I'm finally here, the skinniest boy in school. I'm going to die here, man, I am going to freaking die here . . .

In Hattiesburg black kids got bussed to white schools starting in seventh grade, but white kids didn't get bussed to the black schools until ninth grade. My first morning at Lillie Burney, following the pledge, we were greeted over the PA by our black principal, Mrs. Bonaparte, who told us what an exciting year we had in store. Upon reaching the end of a cloying list of extracurricular activities, she paused to clear her throat and then began to rail against all you thugs, hoodlums, and juvenile delinquents who come here even thinking about scaring my white kids with your shenanigans. I sat straight in my desk to stare up at the box speaker.

"You do, I'll find you out," she warned. "I'll find you out, catch you up, thrash you good, then hand you to the po-lice. You hear me, you thugs, you hoods, you little criminals who don't even belong in a decent school?—I'll hunt you down and send you to jail." She cleared her throat and reverted to her original cloying tone. "Now y'all have a nice day."

The things I witnessed during Mississippi integration still harrow me. Kids getting run over by cars during fights. Students fucking and masturbating in class while teachers slept off hangovers. Kids with exploded bladders being carted into ambulances. I saw countless fights with guns, knives, and arrests. My first week in ninth grade, while I was waiting for the bus home, two black girls attacked each other with razor blades, a fight that ended with the smaller girl having her face slashed open. She fell to the sidewalk while the taller girl kept shredding her back in long red stripes. Nobody stopped this.

That year I drew a sixth-period gym class with only one other white kid in it. The coach was also white, a lummox ex-center at Southern Mississippi with turtle-lidded eyes who always carried a tennis-ball can to spit tobacco juice into. In spite of his size, Coach Kennedy seemed terrified of his students, and as soon as he got some game started in the gym he would escape outside, at which point I would become a plaything of horror passed around like some lifelike squeeze doll so my full range of terrified expressions and squeals could be explored.

All the kids in gym called me *stickman*, a name conferred on me by Ricky Sylvester, who pronounced it *schtickman*. Ricky was around six two, one ninety. The blue tank tops we all wore in gym made it easy to see the scars on Ricky's right biceps, where, rumor had it, he'd been stabbed by his own father. Ricky seemed to be composed of rumors, including the one that claimed he was a good enough musician to be a professional drummer. He carried around drumsticks everywhere he went and could play the opening of the

Commodores' "Brick House" against the bleachers in the gym. I watched him do this in awe. It was like a magic trick to me. The year before, all the white kids had been listening to KISS, but vomiting blood from a stomach ulcer couldn't compete with Lionel Richie's slow-dance voice. The album *Commodores Live!* united the school and was all anybody listened to during the weekly bomb threats when we were herded into the parking lot for prolonged smoke breaks. Eventually Ricky would be arrested for calling in those bomb threats. Or at least that was one of the first rumors about why he'd been arrested. Was it true? I don't know. If he'd been cuffed and led away as the Son of Sam serial killer it wouldn't have surprised me. If he'd been helicoptered out of the school parking lot by the Commodores it wouldn't have shocked me. He was the god of ninth grade. And he was a wrathful god.

During spells of bad weather Coach organized boxing smokers in which we donned comically large gloves and fought each other in a ring mapped out with white tape on the gym floor. I was always matched against the one other white kid in gym. Stevie Halcomb was my opposite, a gym rat who hustled psychotically in basketball. The black kids called him *spidahman* because of how he crouched down on defense. And he would play defense against anybody, even Ricky, which was a foolish thing to do. The one time I'd stolen the ball from Ricky he'd wheeled around and knocked me unconscious. The other kids dragged me off the court and kept playing.

Stevie took no pleasure in boxing me silly in our smokers. If anything, it seemed to embarrass him. Because I was so comically awkward, a stick figure in padded gloves, the kids serving as ring ropes always rooted for me—*get 'em schtickman!* —as they launched me back into the ring while Coach slunk outside to empty his spit can.

The series of events that led to Stevie's disappearance started the day I got smashed in the face with a volleyball during a game called King's Court, a sadistic incarnation of dodgeball using ten diseased volleyballs—all underinflated to make them palmable. I'd spun around to avoid one ball only to be nearly decapitated by another. After doing a backflip midair and being somewhat revived, I was sent by Coach to fetch the first aid kit for myself, an errand that in itself seems impossible to explain.

The locker room I entered had green cinder-block walls and was filled with cross-shaped wooden benches. Metal baskets containing our street clothes were shelved along the walls. Earlier that fall while we were getting dressed, a small kid named Dereker Allan had pulled a pistol out of his basket and started waving the gun around at everybody. Dereker was freaked out because of something Ricky and his friends had done to him earlier that week—I never heard what they did, although I can guess. As Dereker turned circles pointing the pistol at everybody, I sunk to the floor and crannied myself under a bench just in time to see Coach fleeing the room. He locked the door behind him, but we didn't find that out until kids started trying to escape. Luckily nobody got shot—the gun didn't even have bullets. Dereker was arrested, and as far as I know Coach Kennedy was never reprimanded for locking his students inside a small room with an active gunman. And if all this sounds absurd, well, yeah, that's what I'm hoping to convey, the surreal incompetence governing integration in south Mississippi in which bomb threats were a welcomed smoke break, coaches contrived ridiculously violent games to render students broken, teachers slept through classes, and policemen roamed the hallways removing children from desks.

Bleeding from both nostrils, I staggered toward Coach's office holding his monstrous set of keys. I found the door to the locker room unlocked and pushed it open and stumbled down the hall leaving a trail of blood and turned the corner to face the dank room of bas-keted walls. At that point I stood as statue-still as any human has ever stood. My nose, however, continued to drip blood onto the tile floor. It sounded like a basketball being dribbled very slowly.

In front of me, two kids were holding Stevie Halcomb from behind so that he faced Ricky Sylvester, who was standing on a bench. Ricky had pulled his dick out from underneath his gym shorts and started pushing it into Stevie's face. Had Ricky looked up, he would have spot-ted me standing under the exit sign. Two steps backward and one to the side and I would be out of his line of vision, but I couldn't move.

"Don't cry on my dick, Spidahman," was the only thing I heard Ricky say. He said it almost tenderly. The noise Stevie made a moment later didn't sound like crying, it sounded like choking to death. I closed my eyes and tried to take a step backward but couldn't. I felt like a helium balloon that might pop or float into the sky. I wasn't even breathing. When I opened my eyes again, Ricky was staring right at me. He pinned me there with his sedated grin, as if pleased to have an audience. In a fit of brilliance I grinned back at him, then, almost casually, I turned and walked down the hallway and followed the trail of blood I'd left there. I did not run. I'd already learned that the more frightened you were the slower you should move. While walking away I noticed the fire alarm mounted on the cinder-block wall. I knew I should pull it, I wanted to help Stevie, but I couldn't. Ricky would know.

I skirted across the breezeway into the gym, snatched a dirty towel from the bin, and held it to my nose as I climbed onto the bleachers and sat under a helicopter headache watching kids destroy each other in King's Court. While doing this, I began to rock back and forth—a habit that would follow me for years to come. While rocking, I watched as the two kids who had held Stevie's arms rejoined the game. When Stevie returned, he sat a few rows below me on the bleachers and held his face in his hands. Coach came over and said something to Stevie, who stood, nodded a few times while blinking wildly, and then collapsed fetal onto his side and started throwing up onto the court. When he quit vomiting, Coach sent him to the nurse's office. Stevie never returned to gym after that, and for the rest of the year I was the only white kid in class.

Sad to say, Stevie's rape worked out well for me. From that day forward I became Ricky Sylvester's pet. Every time we passed each other in the hall, he'd curl back his lips to say *schtickman* with relish and then hold out his palm for me to slap. In gym he stopped other kids from tormenting me. For half a year, until his arrest, Ricky was my guardian angel.

The last time I saw Ricky he was being cuffed in the hallway. Over the next week I heard a half-dozen rumors as to why he'd been arrested, everything from drugs to armed robbery to bomb threats to murdering his own father. Years later I learned he'd been murdered in Parchman. Upon hearing that, I instantly remembered how he would flash that grin at me in the hallway and hold out his hand. And each time we slapped hands, I felt his power pass into me.

As to Stevie, I didn't notice him again until the next year at an equally derelict school called Rowan when he got into a fistfight with Dereker Allan. They were the same size and went at it inside a blur of roundhouses, the fight ending when Stevie's nose exploded, his blood flying onto my shirt. After Stevie went down, Dereker mounted his chest and started pummeling his face. With teachers approaching, Dereker picked Stevie up and launched him headfirst into a sticker bush, and that was the last time I ever saw Stevie.

I bank hard left in my fluttering wingsuit and travel back upstate over the ocean of pine until I spot the glistening whiteness of Gentry and swoop down through the sunroof of the ebony Town Car motoring down the highway as if in a commercial, and once behind the wheel I pause to take a long, refreshing sip of my delicious Red Bull.

# WINDY REACH

After forty minutes of bouncing around town, I'm almost caught up and starting to think, okay maybe I've survived the worst, maybe I won't even get called back to Miguel's. Then the phone rings and it's a number I don't know, but I sure as hell recognize the voice.

"You gotta come get me, dawg. I just texted you my address."

"What are you doing in town, Tony?"

"Just come get me. Get me out of here. Please."

With that, he hangs up.

Please? Tony just said *please*? Holy shit, the world's gone mad. I call Horace and tell him what just happened.

"He said *please*," I add.

"Well go get him," Horace snaps.

"But I gotta go to Kroger. Then campus. Man, you been running me coast-to-coast all day. I'm like a goddamn badminton . . . thing."

"I'll get those two, you get Tony."

Thing is, Horace knows that Tony will call him next, and the last thing Horace wants is Tony wiping boogers in the Suburban.

"Shuttlecock," I say five minutes later, still batting at cobwebs.

While driving toward Tony, I begin to wonder if I am aiding and abetting again. After all, I know he's on the lam for attempted murder, right? Aghast at the thought of sharing a jail cell with Tony, I close the sunroof of the cab and turn up the AC full blast gas mileage be damned. The address he texted is ten minutes south of town on Ross Barnett Road. As usual he has texted me the wrong address—that's all he ever did as a dispatcher—but as I'm driving toward that wrong address, I spot Tony standing on the shoulder of the road.

He gets in front. One look and I can tell, as impossible as it seems, that he's been weeping.

"What are you doing here, Tony?" I ask at the end of our first mile together.

"I had to see her, you know? So I cut off my ankle monitor and hitchhiked down."

He begins picking his nose after saying this. For some reason that makes me feel more grounded.

"You hitchhiked to Mississippi? From, like, Kansas?"

He nods gloomily. Still picking.

"Where are we going? The Rebel?"

He nods again. We fall quiet. Then, at the end of the second mile, I clear my throat and ask who it was he needed to see so badly.

"Cheryl," he replies.

Cheryl? You remember her? The completely normal completely attractive woman with the all-American kids who for unfathomable reasons allowed Tony to repeatedly fuck her with a used condom?

"Wait. You broke off a police monitor thing and hitchhiked all the way down here to see . . . Cheryl?"

He nods a few more times and says, "I had to try and explain things to her, you know?"

I keep glancing at the Shakespeare air freshener to test whether this is a dream. I figure if it's a dream then the air freshener will change into a different poet each time I look at it. But it keeps being Shakespeare. As I'm doing this, it's slowly registering in my brain that Tony has performed the single most romantic act of any man since Romeo drank poison. Tony was willing to get sent to prison in order to see this woman and explain his side of the story about how he forgot to mention he was wanted by the law and has three kids by another woman and doesn't really own All Saints Taxi. He was risking that prison rape scene to tell this woman in so many words that he loves her.

"So . . . how'd that go?" I ask during the third mile.

He shakes his head as if trying to dispel a fly.

"Was a disaster."

"That was Cheryl's place back there? This just happened, now—that's why you called me to come get you?"

He nods and I continue to frown at Shakespeare until this tic thing starts vibrating my right eyelid. Like it's being electrocuted. I clamp my hand over my eye and keep driving.

"Hey you mind we make a stop?" Tony asks.

I pout for a moment but then shrug.

"Sure, man. It's been that kinda day. Where to?"

He says his mom's house and instantly a million questions roil my mind. It even occurs to me that Tony might be planning to rob Stella. She does have a safe, or so I've heard, but surely she wouldn't be stupid enough to give Tony the combination.

"Okay," I reply, once again bewildered by his ability to get me to take him to places I don't want to go.

Stella lives out on 9 west in one of those aging suburbs with a man-made lake where all the houses are these identical gray-brick numbers with eyelike awnings over their upstairs bedrooms. Aside from small details such as a basketball hoop in the driveway or a sapling in the front yard it's all the same house. I'm remembering the drug houses we visited together as I pull into the entrance and pass a sign that says WINDY REACH. I'm remembering how Tony told Stella we were friends.

"There—stop," Tony says with his familiar impatience. "Don't use the driveway."

We park on the street and he rolls down the window and stares at his mother's house. Like he's trying to get up his nerve for something. Robbery, for instance.

"She knows you're in town," I tell him. "She's been worried about you."

The face he gives me says otherwise. It says nobody's worried about me, not Cheryl, not even my own damn mother. He lets me have five seconds of that baleful face before turning it back upon the house where he grew up. I'm praying Stella doesn't open the door and see us. I'm not sure what Tony is trying to get up his nerve to do right now, but it can't be good, can it? No, it can't be.

"You know she gutted my old man, right?"

Huh? I have no idea what he's talking about. The words make no sense. My brain is deceased inside its little brain coffin.

"It was self-defense. I guess."

I'm still confused, still waiting for that little lightbulb to flicker on. Gutted? Self-defense? I just want to shut my eyes and breathe myself to death. It would be so easy to do. Oblivion. Yeah, I need some of that.

"She had a fishing knife stashed under her pillow. He was knocking her around . . . supposedly. At least that's what she told the cops afterwards. He was drunk. He hit her. So she, you know, gutted him."

Tony makes a motion like ripping up somebody's insides with a knife, and suddenly everything makes sense, and I say, "Oh."

Then I say oh again. Then I say oh *God*.

He's still staring at the house.

"There?" I ask. "In there?"

"In there. We didn't even move afterwards."

I think about ghosts. I think about the ghost of Tony's father walking around this neighborhood with his guts trailing out. It must be confusing to a ghost how all these houses look alike. I imagine him dragging his guts house to house haunting the wrong people while trying to find the bitch who killed him. I want to ask Tony if he's ever seen his father's ghost. Instead I look at the house some more. I look at each window. I'm afraid I'm going to see a face staring back at me.

I ask Tony how old he was when it happened.

"Wasn't," he says. "She was six months pregnant with me."

"Oh. Jesus."

I think about that. About being part of the body that killed your own father. I wonder does that make Tony an accomplice.

"Never heard anybody say a good word about him."

My mind gives up. I shake my head, close my mouth.

"Fuck this. Let's get outta here, Tony," I hear myself say.

A long moment passes before he nods.

As we leave Windy Reach and turn left onto the highway, my phone starts ringing.

"It's your mom."

"Don't tell her I'm here."

I answer on the Bluetooth.

"Yeah, he is," I tell her. "He's okay."

I'm afraid to lie to Stella now. It feels like I'm talking to a different person, a Stella who might gut me.

"Okay, I will," I say.

I take the earpiece out, toss it in my tip cup.

"She says for you to call her."

He nods again. I notice a tear streaming down his cheek and look away. The road blurs.

When we reach the motel, Tony takes a handgun out of his waistband and asks if I want to buy it. It's sleek and black and not a cowboy revolver like Moondog's so it must be an automatic. A nine, maybe? God, I hate handguns. I hated them even before Dereker Allan pointed one in my face at gym. Tony's turning the gun over like he's the one considering buying it. Now I'm wondering if he was planning to murder his mother while we were parked at the house.

"Put that thing away, man."

"Just make me an offer, dawg."

"I don't want a gun. Wait—you didn't kill Cheryl, did you?"

"What? Why would I kill Cheryl?"

I can tell from the anger in his voice that he's telling the truth.

"Sorry. It's just that, I dunno, I really hate guns."

"What's wrong with your eye, G?"

I will never admit this to anyone else, but I kind of like being called G.

"I don't know." I keep pressing my fingers to my eye and then testing my hand away to see if the lid will stop vibrating. "Maybe I'm having a stroke."

"Just take the damn thing, okay? Otherwise I'm going to shoot myself with it as soon as I walk into that fucking room."

As I gaze into his chimp eyes, I know he is sincere about that, too.

"Take it—it's yours. You're saving my life here."

He's holding the gun out to me, but I won't take it.

"Why do you even have a gun, Tony?"

Admittedly, it's not the most intelligent question to ask a fugitive. For all I know, Tony's been armed every day he's been in my car.

"I let Cheryl borrow it. She thought she saw some perv spying in her bedroom window and it freaked her out. Actually it was me spying in her window. I thought she was fucking her ex again. I lent her the gun so she wouldn't think it was me, right?" He taps at his temple. "She said I was chiva—"

"Chivalrous."

"Yeah. I had to look that one up. I knew it meant something good because she gave me a blow job that night. It's a lucky gun, dude. Take it."

I take the gun because I'm afraid he might start weeping. I seriously do not want Tony weeping in my cab. If he does, I'll start weeping too.

I set the gun between us on the bench seat.

"I was right, too."

"Right about what?"

"About her ex. They're getting back together. Because of the kids. She said she still loves me but has to do what's best for the kids."

"She said she still loves you?"

The incredulousness in my voice is lost on him.

He nods solemnly, sniffs.

"But she said that doesn't matter—that we can never get back together. Being with me would make her lose custody."

"I'm sorry, man."

"Women are so weird."

"Yeah."

"Why don't you like guns? I thought all dudes liked guns."

"I'm not sure. Maybe because my grandfather killed himself with one."

"Your grandfather shot himself?"

"Yeah. My father told me about that when I was six. Who the hell tells a six-year-old kid that kinda bullshit? I mean, I didn't even know what suicide meant until my dad explained it to me that day. Man, that was fucked up."

"Why'd he shoot himself?"

"I don't know, man. Suicide runs in my family. All the men kill themselves, and all the women die of strokes. Anyway, ever since the day my dad told me that shit about my grandfather it was like . . . I dunno, like suicide became my new best friend. Like he was always there beside me." I catch myself, then fake laugh, then add, "Which is why I shouldn't have a gun. Seriously."

"But you gotta take it. If I get caught hitching with it, God knows where they'll send me. Remember that story I told you? About Rikers? About my friend who—"

"Yeah. I remember."

And suddenly I think about Althea and wonder is she's still alive. She hasn't called for a ride in weeks. Who's taking her to dialysis?

Tony picks up the gun, kisses it goodbye, and sets it back on the bench seat so that it's pointing at my kneecap. Seeing my reaction to that makes him smile for the first time.

"Relax. The safety's on."

"You mean it's loaded?"

"Duh. Full clip."

He leaves it there and gets out of the cab. Then, before shutting the door, he squats down to ask if he can borrow twenty bucks. I reach into my kitty and hand him three twenties. He stuffs them into the pocket of his jeans.

"Hey, man, thanks. Thanks for being nice to me. All the other drivers hate my guts. They all treat me like shit—just 'cause I owe them money."

I cough a few times while staring at the gun. Then I nudge the barrel until it's pointing toward the back seat.

"If you're leaving now," I tell him, "I can give you a ride to the highway."

"No. I need to get some sleep. I been up for three days straight. Four? Three? I dunno. What does it matter?"

When I ask what's going to happen to him, Tony shrugs again, like that doesn't matter, either, like who the hell cares?

"My lawyer says it'll go easier on me if I turn myself in. He said to make sure they don't know I crossed a state line."

My back is aching and I get out of the car to stretch. Then I reach my arm across the roof of the cab and we shake hands and I tell him good luck. It's possible that I mean it. Probably not, though. I've hated him for so long. I've hated him in my dreams.

"Don't tell nobody what I told you," he says.

I nod and get back inside the cab beside my lucky gun.

Then Tony is gone.

Thinking that, and being grateful for it, I wrap the gun inside a towel and place it under my seat. That's where all the other drivers keep theirs. Now I'm like every other saint in Stella's heaven. Now I'm Lucky Gun Lou.

# DISCOMBOBULATED GHOSTS

The crickets in my head sound like frogs now. I'm parked in the motel parking lot sitting on a gun and trying to think of the most romantic thing I've ever done. But I'm stymied. I feel so odd, so light-headed, so froggy, that I'm starting to worry that maybe it wasn't an Adderall I took. Maybe it was some other pill? I can't move. I'm stuck here at the motel, just staring at Tony's yellow door. Meanwhile the hipsters are milling about setting up their paintings for tonight's art hop. They decorate the rooms extravagantly, as you'd expect artists to do. It must confuse the motel ghosts terribly. Every night they slit their wrists at the same time in the same room surrounded by the same décor, and now suddenly there's this giant painting of Jimi Hendrix hung on the wall next to some LSD-inspired exoplanet. Those poor discombobulated ghosts.

I sit there thinking about the grandfather I never met. My grandfather worked for the Baseball Hall of Fame all his life. When I was thirteen, long after his suicide, my dad took me to visit the Hall of

Fame, and while we were driving through Cooperstown he pointed to a motel—some seedy dive not much different from the Rebel—and said, "That's where my old man did himself."

I sigh and get out of the cab again and plod across the lot and knock on the faded red door while imagining the two women inside cowering in a corner terrified at hearing the two knocks on the door, looking at each other, wondering, is it him, is it *Jase come to kill us?* As hard as it is to fathom, this is the drug-rush moment some men live for, the spell they cast that makes women tremble in fear of them. The meth twins don't answer, nobody's home—or if they are home, they're too afraid to open the door. I yell out it's me, Lou, *your* cabdriver. After waiting a few more minutes I limp back to the cab with one hand clamped over my twitchy right eye, the other eye scanning the motel, searching for friends, for enemies . . .

Aside from the painters, not much is shaking at the Rebel. Cancer Max is nowhere to be found, but even remembering the taste of his pizza gets my Spidey sense vibrating morosely. There's no way I'm surviving today, I realize. This is it. The day the five million Shakespeares of bad karma finally contrive to kill me. I don't even care, man. Like Hamlet going into suicide-by-cop mode, I am resigned to my fate. Poison me. Stab me. Whatever. See if I care.

I remove my hand, and my eyelid instantly starts twitching again.

I'm about to write the meth twins a note warning them about Jason when Horace calls me. How does he know I've become vacant? He is either a clairvoyant or a Satanist. Maybe they all are, I decide. Maybe All Saints Taxi is an ironically named satanic cult that meets secretly in the woods to sacrifice possums and armadillos on makeshift altars. I imagine them standing in the torchlit dark wearing blood-red hoods with Stella presiding. Mississippi Satanists are the worst, man. I know this firsthand because I grew up living in fear of them. We were always told they were performing sacrifices in the woods surrounding our town. What a strange way to grow up. You're not a Mississippian, I guess, unless you've spent the long nights of childhood terrified that Satanists are climbing the sides of your house like iguanas toward your bedroom window. Fuck Horace, I decide. Fuck Stella. I let the phone ring and concentrate on the eyelid fluttering beneath my palm. Meanwhile my mind, or what's left of it, is trying to remember one goddamn fucking romantic gesture I might have made in my horribly misspent life.

Finally I give up and pick up the phone.

"Go get Teddy at Miguel's," Horace says.

And I do. Like Hamlet wading into his fatal joust, I drive to Miguel's and wait, and wait. Fifteen minutes later the glass door opens and two couples come faltering out of the restaurant. If you didn't know better you might think them human. But they are not human. They are alien freak shows from planet Stepford. I know this because I have just put on my knockoff *They Live* sunglasses and can see quite clearly they aren't human, they aren't us.

The retired senator and his doddering wife are extremely sodden, but they are not nearly as inebriated as Tiff and Teddy. Over dinner it has been decided that the senator will leave his BMW at Miguel's, and I will taxi everyone home. Their party slur-spills into my cab and starts lighting cigarettes. Then, just as we're about to embark, Tiff suggests that we lock the senator's BMW before we leave. That Tiffany has made a practical suggestion is in itself evidence that some diabolical plan, sent by an angry cosmos, has begun. In her own way Tiff has answered all my questions about karma and God. It makes no sense that Tiffany would suggest we lock the BMW. The universe is showing its hand with this impossible-to-believe detail. That's my gut feeling here.

I stare at Tiff in the rearview as if to ask how did that come out of your mouth? Why did you pick this moment to say something reasonable?

The senator's wife begins to search for her keys, which of course are nowhere to be found. The senator then begins to yell at his wife for having lost the goddamn car keys. Now Tiff breaks character again by defending an old lady from her bullying husband—up is down, right is wrong, a world pulled inside out—and soon Tiff and the senator are screaming at each other so loudly it awakens Teddy, in the passenger seat beside me, who immediately lights a cigarette and then drops it onto his lap. It is burning through the crotch of his high-water khakis yet he is too drunk to realize his dick is on fire. Everyone in the back seat keeps screaming, a full-blown opera, except for the senator's wife, who is weeping and fumbling through her purse when the senator orders Tiff to go back inside and look for the keys, to which Tiff heroically replies, "Why don't you go find them your fucking self? Or send this sack-of-shit son of yours to do something useful for once in his life."

Am I becoming a fan of Tiffany's? First Tony and now Tiff? There are no rules anymore. I sip my Red Bull while Tiff staggers inside the restaurant to look for the keys. When I glance over again, the cigarette has magically returned to Teddy's mouth. Or maybe he lit a new one. It's quiet in the car, although I am expecting Teddy to start bellowing at any moment and suspect it might be that groinal cry that kills me.

Tiff returns holding a bottle of wine in a brown paper sack, which she raises victoriously over her head with a grin before getting back into the car.

"Can you believe we almost forgot this!" she says once inside.

"What about the keys?" I ask.

"The keys? Oh, they weren't there."

"Did you ask the busboy?"

My question is ignored and within seconds they are all screaming at each other again. I put the car in gear while studying their grotesque faces in the rearview. In this mind-set I drive toward the senator's house with my passengers wailing at each other. Inside this din Stella calls me. I answer but don't say anything, just hold up the phone and let her absorb the cachinnations of alien madness. Tiff, in the back seat, is now hitting Teddy in the front seat with her little fists. The bobbing effect this creates makes it appear that Teddy is enjoying music, following the rhythm of some inner song. He is sitting alone in the front because everyone was afraid he would start vomiting on them.

"Make him get up there with the driver," the senator had ordered when they piled in.

As I turn into the heavy traffic on Vardaman Avenue, the Town Car issues a pathetic groan—like a sperm whale struck by a harpoon—and suddenly we are lowriders, suddenly the world is too tall and our asses feel to be dragging blacktop. I pull into the nearest lot and get out and walk around the car. I can still hear them screaming at each other inside. Have they even noticed we are stopped? I consider leaving them there and calling a taxi.

The problem, I ascertain, is that the rear suspension has collapsed. This has been remedied in the past by flipping a switch in the trunk that reactivates the air shocks, which are the Achilles' heel of the Town Car. I flip the switch. Nothing. I flip it again. Nothing. The wheels are almost brushing the wells. I get back inside and slowly continue our journey. Driving from this low vantage point makes me feel like a child. First we drop off the senator and his weeping wife. By the time we arrive back at Teddy's house I find myself unable to speak. Maybe I've had a stroke. It's hard to say. Anyway I feel weird. Indifferent, I guess. My eye has stopped twitching but something's wrong with my ears now. Things sound strange. Deeper. Slower. Plus there's this layer of demonic peepers.

"Is he okay?" Tiff asks Teddy.

We are parked in their driveway, but I have no idea where we are or how we got here. Why is the world so tall? Teddy wands his hand in front of my face trying to get my attention. They call out to me and try to cull me from my cave, but I do not emerge. At one point Teddy waves a hundred-dollar bill before my eyes and starts crooning the words *cooold beeeer*. Eventually he gives up and drops the bill into my lap.

Then they are gone.

I sit there in the driveway. It's a beautiful day and there are sparrows splashing in a cement birdbath but I am not attracted to them. There's a German shepherd taking a quivering dump in the neighbor's yard but I am not repulsed. Bird chirp. Dog yap. Car horn. A seashell hum blends with the frogs yet I can hear everything around me clearly. It's all music. It's all a type of music.

I'm still riding this wave of indifference when Tiff comes slouching back outside. She collides into the hood and then hobbles to the door and slurs *forgot m' fuckin lighter* as she slides into the front seat and starts groping me. I let her do whatever she wants. I'm still listening to the music of the universe as she kisses my neck, my face, my lips. Then, after probing her tongue into my ear, perhaps even into my brain, she starts unzipping my fly, but I'm not even here. I'm just another ghost in a Town Car that's been parked in a junkyard for decades. I sit there in the junkyard and let her ghost molest my ghost. My hands are still on the wheel as if I am driving. Then Tiff goes back inside. Dispatches keep pinging in. The phone starts ringing. I don't care. I have crawled through the uterus of despair into the womb of samadhi. I just sit there listening to its bittersweet music.

The spell doesn't last long. Just that bug-zap of union before the bubble pops. The anger returns, the jealousy, the fear. They quickly reassemble me.

At which point I realize the hundred-dollar bill in my lap is now gone.

Yeah, Tiff copped my tip while pawing me.

"KILL THEM! KILL THEM ALL!" Goat Man bellows.

I wait until his voice has quit echoing, then I nod obediently, a minion, and get out of the cab and start walking toward the front door. I am going to go Helter Skelter on this house. I can already see the yellow police tape, the bloody hieroglyphs smeared on the walls, when all at once I recall Tony's prison-shower story. The horribleness of that story stops me from going inside and murdering everyone in sight. For that one moment Tony is the Buddha.

I experience some missing time after that and find myself parked downtown in the taxi slot facing the Oasis. The sun is setting behind me and the digital clock indicates my shift has two minutes left. What happened? How did I get here? Was the Town Car abducted? Have I murdered anybody? And why is my fly unzipped? All that matters, I guess, is that I am almost off work. DON'T STARE AT THE CLOCK, MAN! I am staring at the clock when Horace calls and tells me to go pick up this guy David at the organ transplant hospital in Memphis.

Fuck! Fuck-fuck-fuck!

Horace, that brownnosing bastard, loves sending me on last-second runs. Sometimes I suspect he gets the dispatches earlier in the day and waits until the last moment of my shift to call me. At least once a week we argue about this. Stella is aware of the tension between us and has asked me to bear with the situation until she hires this new driver she will never hire.

"Organ transplant hospital? Man, I'm like five minutes from my couch—I've already decided what drink to make—can't you please send somebody else this time?"

My complaint is followed by dead noise. Horace has an economy of words. Finally he mutters, "Just you and me, bro, and I'm dispatchin'. Anyway weren't you complaining to Stella behind my back about not getting enough Memphis runs?"

"Fuck," I say, because he's got me there. Memphis, an hour and fifteen minutes away, is a buck fifty per head—that's seventy-five minus gas plus tip—much better loot than you make windmilling in traffic. Horace tends to hoard Memphis runs for himself or his cronies, especially Kirby. At this point I should just suck it up and head to Memphis, but instead I try to weasel out of the trip by telling Horace I already have to go to Memphis tomorrow morning—my one morning off this week—to pick up a friend at the airport. Horace interrupts to say I'd better not be taking the Town Car to Memphis tomorrow morning.

"I'm not taking the damn Town Car," I whine. "I'm taking a friend's Lexus."

As soon as we hang up, Horace snitches me out to Stella, who calls me two minutes later demanding to know if I'm taking her Town Car to Memphis tomorrow. I tell her no, I'm not taking her precious goddamn Town Car, I'm taking my friend Vance's Lexus to pick him up at the airport.

"He lets me drive his car when he's on vacation."

I'm having trouble speaking now. My words sound post-stroke syrupy. As I talk, or try to talk, I'm imagining Stella smoking her cigar while playing with a knife, maybe doing that mumblety-peg-type game between her fingers. How many men has she killed? I wonder. Where are the bodies?

"Oasis Vance?" she asks me.

I grunt yeah.

"He once told me we charge too much."

I can tell, from the way she said it, that Stella will never forgive Vance this, and I also know that Vance will have no memory what-soever of that conversation.

We do charge too much, I want to tell her. Yet somehow nobody makes any money. We rip people off and don't make shit. Nobody, not even you, Stella. I don't get it.

"How much are you charging him?" she asks me.

"Who?"

"Vance."

"Oh. Nothing. He's a friend. I'm just picking him up at the . . . airport. He's been on vacation in . . . Mexico."

"Don't ever take the Town Car on secret runs. Even in Memphis, I always find out."

". . . secret runs?"

"I'll always find you out." She pauses and then adds with a bit of uncer-tainty, "I have friends. I've been in this business a long time, buster."

And that, I know, is true. Half the people who enter my cab drop her name. She's had a huge impact on Gentry and has gotten thousands of drunks home without them killing anybody. In her own way Stella is a saint who has saved more lives than the average doctor. It's not an easy job—not on any level. Nobody's getting rich and everybody thinks they're getting ripped off. Hell, cabbies still operate on the honor system—no wonder everybody's so paranoid.

"No secret runs, mister," she says again, this time in a lighter tone. Then she adds, "Now I need you to go get Abigail before Memphis."

I don't reply. Again, I'm scared to open my mouth.

My eye starts twitching again.

"I know, I know—but she requested you."

"She requested me?" I reply truculently even though I know it's true. Abigail is the PhD student who Kirby keeps inviting to his hypothetical orgy.

"I'll make you a deal—you can come in an hour late tomorrow afternoon—how's that sound?"

"An hour? I need a whole day off, Stella. I can't do this anymore. I'm losing my mind. Seriously, I feel like I've had a . . . stroke thing. And, look, you gotta get Horace to start—"

"I know, I know—I told you I'm hiring this new guy next week."

"You been saying that for months."

"That's because I am. His name's Ace."

"Whose name is Ace?"

"The new driver I'm hiring."

"Oh," I say dully.

Knowing this lie has a name makes me feel better.

"Now go get Abigail before I get mad," she says and hangs up.

After going spastic with my middle fingers, I go get Abigail. Anyway I like Abigail. She's an MFA graduate who just realized her degree is worthless and has now taken out a new student loan to enter the PhD program. She specializes in women in mythology, or fables, or fairy tales—something like that. She was in the army and is kind of small with a buzz haircut and pretty in a bookish way. Her round glasses make her green eyes look huge.

When she gets into the back seat, I ask what's new and she tells me that she's just applied for a grant to fund a feminist literary journal.

I try to listen to her describe this journal, but instead I'm thinking about the gun under my seat and something Kirby once told me. He told me, by way of advice, that every woman who gets into your front seat wants to fuck you. I'm thinking Kirby is what's wrong with the world and maybe I should shoot him with my lucky gun. There's lots of other people I want to shoot as well, but Kirby should be first, I decide.

I'm imagining myself shooting Kirby in the dick as Abigail finishes describing the feminist journal she wants to start.

I hear myself say, "It's like opening a coffeehouse or starting a band."

"What is?"

"Sorry. I'm a little . . . I meant starting your own . . . literary thing . . . magazine, journal, is."

"Hey, you okay, Lou?"

"Yeah, I think I am. I need a day off is all. Where to?"

"Barnett Hall. But first I need to swing by Shipley's to pick up some doughnuts for a meeting."

"Oh," I reply.

Barnett Hall is where I failed so spectacularly at teaching.

I wonder, vaguely, if aging boxers ever reach a point in the late rounds of lost bouts in which they enjoy being hit.

"Have you ever wanted to start your own literary journal?" Abigail asks.

"No. I mean, I've never even read those things. I didn't think anybody did."

"I do."

"Really?"

"Sure. Oh, that reminds me. Are you going to the big reading tonight at Syd's Bar?"

"No, those things creep me out."

Then I ask her who's reading this time.

"Half the English faculty is. I figured you'd be reading tonight too. Here."

She hands me a flyer advertising something called "Noir at the Bar." It's a group reading at Syd's, the only dive bar left in Gentry, and the flyer shows a photocopy of some pulp novel cover—a gangster, a half-naked woman, a gat, a bottle of whiskey—and beneath this picture is a list of the local writers who will be reading—there's about ten of them.

"Stop Us Before We Kill Again!" the flyer says at the top, this headline surrounded by tiny typewriters.

Goat Man attempts a takeover at this point. If there's one thing Goat Man hates it's schoolteacher noir. I shove him back down into the fire lake beside Grendel's mother and finish reading the list of names, the entire MFA faculty. Have any of these writers even worked a night job? Have they ever worked anywhere outside academia? Christ, no wonder regular people don't read anymore.

"Must be like the wild West up in that English department," I mutter.

Then I close my eyes a moment to let Goat Man scream and sputter.

"HELICOPTER PARENT NOIR!" he yowls at me.

"They really didn't ask you to read tonight?"

"KILL THEM! KILL THEM ALL!" he screams.

I hand the flyer over the seat back to Abigail.

"First I've heard of it," I say.

"Wow. That sucks. Hey, what's up with your eye?"

"I'm not sure, Abigail. It's kind of a new development type thing."

The moment I drop her on campus, Stella calls me again.

"Change of plans," she announces in the cheerful voice she reserves for bad news.

"What?—did Memphis cancel?" I ask hopefully.

"No, you still need to get David at that hospital—oh, before I forget, you need to call him first."

"But—"

"Let me finish. Call and get his credit card info before you leave. He's kind of sketchy."

"Sketchy?"

"You know the type."

"I do?"

"Yeah. He'll get away with what he can get away with. One of those."

"Oh. Okay."

The electric wave of déjà vu makes me suspect we've had this conversation before. Maybe we have it every day.

"But I need you to do me a favor first."

"No," I snap. Then I change that to "Oh no." Then I change that to "What?"

"It'll be good money, I promise. I want you to pick up this woman—um, Samantha—from the rehab center and drop her off in Memphis before you pick up David at the hospital there. She needs to go to the airport."

"Which one?"

"There's only one airport in Memphis, dear."

"No. Which rehab? Not the one on 315, I hope?"

"Yeah. The one on 315."

"Oh no."

"Don't worry. She seemed fine on the phone. A bit impatient maybe. Anyway I thought you'd be happy to get a fare both ways. Double your pleasure."

"Huh?"

"It's a commercial. For Doublemint."

I have no idea what we are talking about.

"I think I've had a stroke."

"She's normal, I promise."

"Nobody from that place has ever been normal. They're always jumping out windows and shit."

"Yeah, well, she needs a ride to Memphis, dear, and that's where you're headed. I already let David know you'd be delayed."

"David?"

"The guy at the organ-swap hospital."

"Oh. Sketchy David. Where is that anyway? I thought I knew every hospital in Memphis."

"Must be new. Ask him for directions when you get his credit card numbers. Hey, at least you get to sleep late tomorrow."

"No, I don't. I already told you I'm driving to Memphis tomorrow morning."

"Not in my Town Car, you aren't."

I start to explain that we've had this conversation. At least I think we have—I'm pretty sure we have—but instead I sigh loudly and hope that suffices.

"You're not taking the Lincoln, right?"

"I'm taking Vance's Lexus."

"Oh, okay. You know he once told me we charge too much?"

It feels like I'm standing in an ant bed of déjà vu. I try to sigh again but end up burping.

"We do charge too much," I hear myself telling Stella. "But we're all broke. I just don't get it, Stella. Why aren't you rich?"

"I don't get it either, Lou."

"Where am I going now? You know, like, right now?"

"Gas. Then 315. To the sketchy rehab."

"Oh, yeah. Shit. Sketchy rehab."

"Then sketchy David."

On my way to get gas, I pass Syd's Bar, where the noir gig is being held later tonight. For a moment I imagine myself walking into the bar holding Tony's gun, firing a few shots into the ceiling, then screaming, "HEY, DID ANY OF YOU MOTHERFUCKERS ORDER SOME GODDAMN NOIR? YOU SCHOOLTEACHERS WANT SOME NOIR, HUH?" I press the muzzle or whatever it's called to my temple. "I'LL GIVE YOU SOME FUCKING NOIR!"

It's a brief fantasy, just a momentary rearing of a goat head above the waves, but it illustrates the point that once you have a gun in your possession your mind immediately starts spinning out scenarios that will allow you to employ it. What should I do with this thing? There is simply no way I should be sitting on a loaded gun. If I keep it, I'll probably end up killing myself with it within a year. Or maybe Miko will use it to murder me in my sleep. Is the gun valuable? Has it ever been used in a crime? Has it ever killed anybody? Could I unload it without shooting myself in the dick? Can I just throw it out the car window and be done with it?

The truth is I'm scared to even touch it.

And a darker truth is that I like the feeling of power it gives me.

I fill up on gas and drive home to grab a bite before heading to the rehab. The only thing that's changed at home is that Miko has miraculously moved from the bed to the couch. For her that's like summiting Everest.

She looks up from her book and says hi in a deflated tone.

I nod warily and walk toward the kitchen but then stop myself. Feeling increasingly divided, like a part of me is rummaging through the refrigerator while another part is standing by the couch, I hear myself say, "This has gone on too long, Miko. I need you out of my life. I'm going to stay at Vance's till you're gone. Miko—don't look at me like that—can't you see we're killing each other here? We're like a suicide pact."

After I'm done saying this—I can't believe I actually said it—I think about the gun again. I wonder if it's the gun that has given me the courage to break up with Miko. Maybe I'm a new person now that I have a gun. Now I'm Lucky Gun Lou, and all the rules have changed, and my life is about to get much better.

Or much worse.

"You are such an asshole," Miko says.

The venom with which she says that makes me think she might throw her book at me. The book she might throw at me is called *Les Femmes Illustres* by Madeleine de Scudéry. Miko can read both French and Italian, but, weirdly, she can't speak either of them. It has crossed my mind more than once that she might be lying about her ability to read French and Italian.

"We're killing each other, Miko." I can't even meet her unblinking eyes as I mutter this maudlin line. "Look, I'm sorry, about everything, but I want you out by the end of the month."

"Where am I supposed to go?"

"You must have thought that through by now. You're smart. You knew this was coming. You must have a plan."

Women always have plans, don't they? It's men who never have plans.

I start stepping backward toward the front door. I desperately want her gone. But I even more desperately want myself gone. This isn't a love story, it's a prison break. I should have done this years ago. I'm thrilled I'm finally doing it now, but it's also like a dream of freedom that might pop at any moment.

"You're insane!" she screams at me.

Since I've basically been channeling a handgun for the last few minutes, I don't bother denying this. I just stand at the door and take her wrath. It doesn't matter. I know she will say anything to hurt me now. It's happened so many times before. Soon she's screaming hysterically, and I just keep standing there taking it. I once saw Bob Dylan in concert at Memphis. During the first set he played all his standards and was utterly miserable. After each song, he just stood there wincing into the applause. That's how I feel now as I stand there enduring Miko's wrath like it's a dark wind.

"I should never have come here! You ruined my life! You're fucking delusional. You need to see a shrink. You made this up, Lou, just like you make everything up. Just like you made up that kid Stevie Halcomb so you wouldn't have to deal with what happened to you at school."

We've had variations of this argument so many times that it feels like I'm walking through a series of rooms, one door after another, and in each room I enter Miko and I are having the same argument.

"It wasn't Stevie got raped, it was you. That's why Ricky was so nice to you afterwards. Because you were his bitch. It was you in the locker room. You left your body that day for the first time. You divided yourself—that's not a normal thing to do. You're the one got raped, Lou. You've been suffering PTSD since you were in ninth grade, you idiot, and you need to see a shrink or you are going to die. It's a miracle you've lived this long."

I smile maliciously and start to tell her she's crazy, but then I remember I've already told her that two hundred times before. A feeling of serenity starts to envelop me. This is almost over. I've done it. I've exorcised Miko.

"Listen to me," I tell her. "All that matters is you have to leave here by the end of the month. If you're still here then, I will pick you up and put you outside."

While saying this, I can't help but think how we were happy once, for a little while, how I was so proud of having her as a girlfriend, how I used to tool around town with her on the back of my Vespa.

"I *am* going to be here," she insists, "and you *are* going to have to throw me out. And when you do, maybe I'll go live with the frat boys. I bet they'd like that."

This is another trope. She's got this thing about the frat boys and is always trying to make me jealous over them. Because they are young and beautiful like she is. It used to work, too. I used to get so jealous over them. I mean, for all I know she's been wandering over there every day while I'm tooling around town earning the rent money.

She starts yelling again, calling me all the familiar names, but I just walk out of the house and sit on my lucky gun and after a while I drive away.

# GRACELAND

When a deer bleeds out, its fluids get solidified by the Mississippi sun into a dark red skein on the road. They make great Rorschach tests. It's been such a traumatic day, I'm half expecting a stag to come smashing through my windshield. Fuck it, I decide. I don't even care. I welcome you, stag. There are worse ways to go. Maybe I'll get one of those cool highway crosses that freak everyone out.

Shocked that I finally broke up with Miko—that really happened, right?—I turn onto 315, the Town Car bobbing and lulling, then I call up this guy David at the hospital in Memphis to double-check payment. Right away he gets pissed about having to give me his credit card numbers.

"Hey, you want me to show up or not?" I interrupt him.

After he recites the numbers petulantly, I utter an overly polite goodbye—a trick I've learned from Stella—and hang up. We're off to a bad start, David and me, but who cares? I am sitting on a loaded gun, after all. Don't fuck with me, I think. Don't fuck with me.

Twenty minutes later I turn onto a private road that snakes through pine into the whitewashed rehab complex. Halfway into that maze I hit the brakes. There's a woman in a tie-dye shirt and jeans sitting cross-legged on a boulder surrounded by white garbage bags. For a moment she seems otherworldly, like a goddess straddling her haphazard planet with its orbit of lumpy white moons. Once the brakes have quieted, I roll down the passsenger window and lean across the bench seat to ask if she's waiting for a cab.

"No, I'm communing with nature here, can't you tell? God, what is wrong with you people?"

Her accent is hard to place but definitely not Mississippi. The woman—Samantha, right?—is wearing a Ben & Jerry's tee shirt that I likely tie-dyed in a previous life. I take the shirt as a bad sign. She's younger than me—about forty, I'd guess—her hair a healthy brown fountain spilling without design onto a face that is round and slightly freckled in a mock-wholesome way. I help her load her trash bags into my car. She is amazed at how large my trunk is.

"Hey, what's wrong with this cab? I feel like Shaquille O'Neal here."

I tell her the air shocks deflated, that it happens all the time.

"No big deal," I add.

"No big deal," she repeats in a waning voice. Then, as she is getting into the car, she says, "Samantha Gillespie, when last seen . . ."

Once we're moving—she's in the front seat—I ask if she had to escape out the window.

"Why? Does that happen a lot? Do you know what goes on back there?"

"A little. I mean, I've picked up people here before. At least you got your things. Usually they don't let you have your stuff back if you leave early."

"Jesus, do you think I showed up here with garbage bags? I had to throw my shit out the window. They even kept my iPhone. God knows what they're doing with that. I mean, there's some pretty personal videos on that phone."

"They said they'd ship it to you, right?"

"Yeah. Were they lying?"

"No. I mean, I don't know. I'm just repeating things other people said. I had one passenger who jumped out the window."

"Of your cab?"

"No." I laugh but then stop when it starts sounding spooky. "He jumped out of the, you know, the hospital—the clinic, whatever—um, window. To escape, like." I shake my head. "I've had a long day," I add mysteriously.

"You've had a long day?" she repeats. "Look, mister Mississippi taxi driver, can I please use your cell phone there so I can actually pay you for this ride? I've got to get my husband to transfer money onto my card. I still can't believe what happened to me back there. I'm in shock right now. Don't pay attention to anything I say. Seriously, what is wrong with you people?" She pauses. "You didn't pay any attention to that, right?"

"Right. I take it you're not from around here."

"Hell, no." She crosses herself before picking up my phone with two fingers like it's infected with Ebola. "I might as well be from Mars the way everyone kept staring at me. Chrome? Who the fuck uses Chrome, dude? Mississippi goddamn. Hey, you're not going to take me into the woods and do God knows what to me while some retard plays a banjo, are you? Seriously, what the fuck?"

The moment she says this, I get that *Deliverance* song stuck in my head.

"I'm from West Hollywood," she adds. "Where the stars go to die."

I'm curious about what happened to her in rehab, but my sense is it's better to wait and let it unfurl. Instead of asking her questions, I start searching for deer. It's odd how I can forget about the deer for hours on end and then suddenly I'll get all paranoid and start scouring the roadside for that suicide-bomber buck.

"Hey honey," she says into my phone using a childlike voice. At first I think she's talking to me that way. "Let me speak to your daddy." She waits, then, using a more natural tone, this one resigned and gruff, she says, "Hey Frank. Yeah. I know, you were right. You're always right. I fucked up. Again. Yes, I'm in a cab being driven by an escaped convict with no teeth. Wait. That was a lie probably. Do you have teeth?"

I smile awkwardly, a death-mask grimace.

"Okay, I was wrong about that, too. They're kinda green, but he has teeth." She winks at me like we're confederates. This makes me like her for the first time. It's weird the things that make me like people. "Yeah, if he doesn't strangle me then I'm on my way to the airport in . . . where is it? Mount Pilot? Hooterville?"

"Memphis."

"Hear that? Yes, he sounds normal. God knows where they'll find my body. No. Just don't go there now. It'll be so much more fun to say it to my face. Anyway we're going to be rich once we sue those redneck bastards." She raises her middle finger toward the rearview. "In the meantime—okay—do I have to say it again?—look, I need you to transfer some money. And can you please buy me a ticket on the next flight out of . . . what's the name of the airport?

"Memphis. Memphis International."

"International? You get that, hon? Memphis Inter-*national* in say—" She looks over at me, but I'm still listening to banjo boy.

"How long to Memphis, Billy Clyde?"

Again, I'm a step behind. The sarcastic redneck name throws me off.

"He's had a long day," she says into the phone.

I try, without much success, to estimate our arrival time factoring in the busted shocks, bald tires, and death-scream brakes. Thinking about my tires reminds me I don't have a jack. Usually I borrow Horace's when I get a Memphis run. But it's too late now.

"Hour and a half, if we're lucky."

"My cabbie seems to have no idea, but guesses we'll be there in just over an hour. That is, if he doesn't take me into the woods to dismember me. Seriously, his eyes point in opposite directions." She winks at me again. "Frank, you would not believe what I've been through with these imbeciles. I know, I know, but they told me that they specialized in sex addiction. Not everything is my fault, you know? Doctors aren't supposed to lie to sick people. Look, okay, just transfer the goddamn money so I can pay this poor guy. Otherwise God only knows what he'll do to me. Will you please tell my husband what you'll do to me if he doesn't transfer money into my account?"

She holds the phone toward me.

"God only knows," I say.

She grins. As her grin subsides, her eyebrows slowly rise—she has awesome eyebrows—then she clamps her hand over the receiver to ask me how much.

"How much what?"

"Duh, baby. How much you going to charge me? God, is that fucking Shakespeare? Am I dreaming this?"

"One fifty."

"He says it's two fifty. Plus tip. And—get this—he has a fucking Shakespeare air freshener."

"It's Shakespeare-mint," I whisper.

"You'd tell me if this were a dream, right, hon? God, what if I'm back there in the clinic sound asleep? What if I'm still there?"

While they talk, I put on Beethoven in an attempt to drown out the *Deliverance* soundtrack, but instead it's like Beethoven gets infiltrated by some random inbred banjo. Whatever, I'm going with it. Sex addiction? To my eye she looks too suburban for that. I'd expect tattoos or something. Not that I really know much about sex addicts. Come to think of it, my life has been tragically bereft of sex addicts.

She puts my phone back in its holster.

"He says he's going to transfer the money in fifteen minutes. Is that fucking Beethoven you put on? Beethoven. Shakespeare. Will wonders never cease?"

That confuses me too. The wonders-never-ceasing part. The syntax doesn't make sense to my sleep-deprived brain.

"Hey, is that Bigfoot?"

"Huh? Oh, yeah. It's, uh, wintergreen. No, wait. Shakespeare's winter . . . ah, fuck it."

"We used to call him Big Muddy Man where I grew up."

"Huh? Why would you call Shakes—"

"Not Shakespeare, idiot, Bigfoot."

"Oh. But . . . where are you from?"

"Stratton."

I can't even remember what state that's in, but for some reason it makes me think of Rolling Rock beer and the enigmatic number 33.

"Beethoven in Mississippi? I'm pretty sure you're trying to impress me."

"No. I mean, I put on Beethoven because you got that banjo boy song stuck in my head. You know, *boing-boing-boing-boing*."

She stares at me with spectacular skepticism as I continue to make inexplicable sound effects.

"I'm going to wake up any minute now," she decides and pulls down the sun visor. But right away she pushes it back up and says, "Gawd!—it's a fucking broken mirror, dude!—what are you trying to do to me?" Then she pulls the visor down again and smudges her finger across one eyebrow. Next she examines her finger the way my dad always did after he picked his nose. "It's my own damn fault for being so cheap. They told me they specialized in sex addiction. Back when I was trying to decide which center to go to in order to save my crappy marriage."

Tall cars keep passing my deflated cab, their passengers staring down at us as if we are children.

"But they don't," she adds a minute later.

"Don't what?" I ask in my charming inbred manner.

I turn to look at her—I'm trying to decide how I should react to her inevitable grope when she goes all Tiff on me—and suddenly I'm positive that I really did tie-dye the tee shirt molded around her breasts. The shirt is so tight it appears the tie-dye has been airbrushed onto her nakedness.

"They don't specialize in sex addiction. I was the only one being treated for that. Everyone else was junkies. Who all made fun of me. Well, mostly they just stared at my tits with their mouths open. And they kept making passes at me, too. God, and those accents, I mean, seriously, that's for real? You people really talk that way to each other in private? One guy there had six fingers. Thank God he didn't make a pass at me. Actually he was nice—he's the one who helped me throw my shit out the window. By the way, what took you so long to get there?"

I ask how long she had to wait.

"Hours. The first cab company never showed up at all. The nurses wouldn't even let me back into the office. Finally the one nice person there—the one fucking human being—called you. But it's not like you exactly rushed over, huh?"

"Sorry. But you're in the sticks."

"No kidding? Boing. Boing-boing-boing-boing."

"Don't do that. He really had six fingers?"

She shudders and stares forward with the eyes of a figurehead.

A moment later she whispers, "On each hand."

Once again I've forgotten what we were talking about.

"He had—it was like a little extra pinkie finger, just a stub, growing sideways out of the bottom knuckle of his real pinkie. On both hands."

I close my eyes in order not to imagine that. But I see it anyway. The image develops in my mind like a Polaroid. Then I swerve back onto the road.

"My bad," I say.

"And Jesus God, group therapy—what they called group therapy, was all these men with gorged-out eyes and cracker teeth just staring at me like they expected me to start masturbating at any moment."

After a moment of contemplative silence, I say, "You should have gone to Hattiesburg instead."

"Hattiesburg? What's that?"

"My hometown. South of the state. It's where Tiger Woods went for, you know, sex addiction. It's like the only time Hattiesburg's ever been famous for anything. There was this photograph of Tiger standing on the roof of the clinic huddled over a cigarette looking like he wanted to jump."

"Yeah, well, Tiger can afford it. Though by the time I finish suing those bastards they are going to have to name that place after me. The Samantha Gillespie Institute for the Criminally Hypersexed. Hey, you mind pulling into that store? I need some beer."

*Criminally hypersexed?* I'm thinking as I park. I wonder if beer will make her lose control. I wonder if I want her to. Then I start thinking about sex addiction and decide she probably has some disease. That's how they know they're addicts, right? Maybe she gave it to her husband. Thinking this and other less-than-arousing thoughts, I examine my teeth and eyes in the rearview until Samantha steps outside the convenience store lighting a cigarette. That is definitely one of my Vermont tie-dyes, I conclude. She gets in, removes a Corona longneck from the black plastic bag, and opens it with her lighter. The cap leaps into the back seat like a small acrobat.

"No smoking," I say.

"Fuck you, Billy Clyde," she replies and exhales orgasmically.

I laugh. Again, I like her for her abject rudeness.

"Great selection back there. You want one?"

I say no thanks.

"Hattiesburg, huh? So how come you don't talk like they do?"

I ponder that a moment.

"Too much TV, I guess. When I was a kid I was obsessed with *Bonanza*. You know, the Western. I forced myself to talk just like Little Joe. I was pretty much in love with Little Joe until I hit puberty. Also Davy Jones. God, I'll never love a woman as much as I loved Davy." She studies me clinically as I continue to babble about my relationships with various teen heartthrobs. "And Bobby Sherman. Wow, I'd forgot about Bobby. I had an older sister who raised me on *TigerBeat* magazine. I used to hang their pictures up on my walls just like she did—I'm sure my dad was concerned. David Cassidy. Oh, David. I bet I still know the words to every Partridge Family song."

As soon as I say that, the banjo boy in my head starts plucking out "I Think I Love You" with Beethoven accompanying on piano.

"Is this where you turn down the dirt road and take the chain saw out of the trunk?"

"Trust me, if I had a chain saw it'd be hocked. This is where we hit Highway 55 south. North, I mean. You sure you're going to be able to pay me?"

"Oh. Shit. You mind?"

She takes my phone again and a couple of minutes later reports, "Maybe he's given up on me this time. Maybe he's abandoning me to the natives."

I ease my foot off the gas.

"Please don't. If you kick me out here, I'll end up living in a double-wide with some four-hundred-pound guy in overalls and a bunch of kids with fingers growing out of their eyelids."

I push down on the accelerator in an attempt to dispel that image.

"Fuck it. I'm going to Memphis anyway. You can rip me off if you have to."

I turn down the volume on Beethoven and spy on her until she catches me and gives me the bug eye.

"Quit staring at my tits."

"I wasn't," I say. "I was looking at your shirt. I think I made that shirt. It's called a spider. The tie-dye design is. Basically you fold

spiders just like spirals except you paint one half a solid color then
rainbow the other half in pie slices."

"This? This shirt?"

She gestures down to her airbrushed breasts. I linger there only a
moment before swerving back onto the interstate.

"Yeah. I used to run a teenage sweatshop for Ben & Jerry's. Back
when I lived in Vermont I had the largest tie-dye contract in America—
maybe in the world. I was so overworked it wrecked my marriage plus
it didn't pay shit. I'd underestimated costs when we negotiated the
contract. They knew what they were doing, those hippie bastards.
Yeah, they screwed me over good. Fuck Ben. Fuck Jerry."

"You seem distraught."

I lower my bird finger from the rearview.

"That keeps getting pointed out. I'm okay, I think. It's just that my
Adderall is wearing off."

"Adderall? Ooh, I'd blow a dead cat for an Adderall right now."

Again, I have to close my eyes. Once we're back on the road I tell
her, "I only had the one. I found it on the floorboard."

"You found an Adderall on the floorboard of this cab?"

"Yeah. Happens all the time. It's like these college kids are just
raining prescription drugs."

"And you put it into your mouth?"

I nod. "Also I found this one with it."

I fish the pill out of my pocket and show it to her. As she takes it from
my hand, one of her fingers runs across my palm light as a feather.

"It's green," I point out.

"I see it is."

"Do you know what it is?"

"I will once you give me your phone."

She takes my cell and a few minutes later identifies it as some kind of Xanax knockoff.

"Can I have? Please-please-please."

"Sure, go for it."

She puts it into her mouth, her eyes shutting for that one moment of swallow. It makes her resemble a doll, the way her eyes pop open. Then she remembers the beer and sips from that.

"I love this song," I tell her. "It was found in Beethoven's under-wear drawer after he died. It never even got played while he was alive. It's a bagatelle."

"A bagatelle? What's a bagatelle?"

"I got no idea. I used to know, but now . . ."

My voice tapers off and she lowers the phone as if curious to see what might come out of my mouth next. It's like her eyebrows are daring me on. She waits another beat, just to make sure, then begins pecking at my phone.

"All the flights are full," she announces five minutes later. "Fuck me."

She sets the phone down on her lap in a way that mimics throwing it. Following her hand there, and eyeing the longneck wedged between her thighs, I suggest she try flying standby.

"After what I've been through? Fuck that. I'm going to get a hotel room and a big bottle of whiskey. As soon as my dear husband, who's probably consulting a divorce lawyer right now, comes across with some bread."

"I really wish you weren't wearing that shirt," I tell her.

She gives me another eyebrow dare.

"I didn't mean it that way. It's like I'm having a sweatshop flash-back. Like I'm about to start screaming at teenage girls. *Wear your goddamn masks! Wear your goddamn gloves!*"

"And they never understood why he killed her."

She gets on the phone again. Using her resigned voice, she says, "Sweetie, since there's no seats available, I'm getting a room and a big bottle of whiskey. Just kidding ha-ha. I really am getting a room, though." She shoots me a wink and mimes guzzling from a bottle. "Please send me some money so the cabdriver will stop being mean to me. Otherwise I think he's going to disperse me in the woods. Are you going to disperse me in the woods?"

Again, she holds the phone toward me.

"Anything's possible," I say.

After putting down the phone, she reports, "Ten minutes tops. He said to tell you not to disperse me."

"I'm pretty harmless actually."

"That's what all the great ones say. Hmm, I think I'm going to get drunk in a room at the . . . the Courtyard Marriott? Yes, that sounds perfectly lovely. You don't know what I've been through or you'd never stop consoling me. Send the money, Frank. Goddamnit send the money already." She leans forward to squint at my taxi ID card taped to the dash.

"Lou Bishoff," she says.

"Yep."

"Hawaii?"

"Yep. Fuck Mississippi. I'm a goddamn Hawaiian."

"You were really born in Honolulu?"

"I was. Except my mom—she was from south Mississippi—she hated living on an island and made my father move us back here when I was four."

"Wow. He must have loved her a lot."

"No, not really."

"You're old. Can you remember Hawaii at all?"

"Nah. Well, I can remember one morning walking down Waikiki Beach toward Diamond Head, and there were all these starfish on the sand—all different colors—and my mother told me they were safe to pick up because they were dead. That's what freaked me out and made me remember that day. It was like I suddenly understood the concept of death. All the beautiful starfish were, you know, dead, and I was so sad it . . . anyway, that's my first memory of life on earth." I cough a few times—I'm allergic to cigarettes—then I tell her, "My second memory is throwing up on a plane to Mississippi."

I risk another glance-over. She's staring at her reflection in the side-view mirror and nibbling on the edge of her ring finger. There's no wedding band there. Maybe she hocked it. Or maybe she lost it in some guy's anus. Trying to avoid such thoughts, I make myself think about Hawaii, about the time Miko and I hiked the Na Pali trail together. She sprained her ankle and I had to piggyback her through miles of switchbacks until we arrived at Kalalau Beach, the most beautiful place on earth. The paradise where I wasn't raised.

Oh, Miko. We were happy once, but that was so long ago.

Samantha startles me out of my reverie by saying, "You can read, too?"

She's holding up my paperback, the one about early Buddhism. I look around trying to decide where we are and how long I've been driving on zombie autopilot. My eyes must have stayed open or she would have screamed, right?

"You're a Buddhist?"

"Yeah, kinda. My girlfriend Miko got me interested in Buddhism. Actually she's not my girlfriend anymore. I broke up with her today."

"You broke up with your girlfriend? Today?"

"I told you I've had a hard day. Anyway, I bought that book, because, well, I'm hoping it helps me stop flipping people off in traffic. It's getting to be a problem. One day I'm gonna flip off the wrong dude. We all have guns down here."

"Do you have one?"

"One what?"

"A gun."

I hesitate a bit too long to lie.

"What kind?" she asks.

"A nine," I tell her, which comes out sounding like a question.

"On you?"

"I guess."

"Can I hold it?"

I think about that. It's a complicated moment here, what with the gun purportedly being "lucky." For an instant I imagine Samantha holding the gun while taking me inside her mouth. Then I imagine her pointing the gun and demanding my kitty before potting me in the head.

"That's probably not a good idea," I decide.

"Please. I've never held a real gun before. Can I at least see a picture of it?"

"A picture? Who the hell takes pictures of their gun?"

Then I think about Kirby, who has a miniature replica of his revolver dangling from the rearview of his cab. Just to make sure everybody knows what he's sitting on.

"People take pictures of everything, dude. God, I hope they aren't looking through my phone right now. Does it have a name?"

"Name? What?—does my gun have a name?"

"Yeah. Like the Widow Maker or something."

"The Widow Maker?"

"Something like that. You definitely need to name your gun. It's like having a pet."

"I don't even like guns."

"If you don't like them then why do you have one?"

"Long story. It kinda comes with the car."

"You sure I can't hold it?"

"Yeah, I'm pretty sure."

She mock pouts for the next mile while I search for deer.

"This is such bullshit," she says.

When I look over, she's pointing at something inside the book.

"It says here that everything's impermanent and that even the cells in your body replace themselves every seven years. But that's bullshit. Your brain cells don't replace themselves and neither do the ones in your immune system. They're the same ones you're born with. That's something I learned in Mississippi. That and the medical term *poke hole*."

I can't rally a reply, but while falling back to sleep I think about what she said, about brain cells and memory and dead starfish and poke holes. I dream about Hawaii, about Miko floating naked on the waves off Kalalau. I wake up fast, riveted upright by fear because it's the only time I've fallen asleep and had a dream while driving.

The bank transfer still hasn't come through by the time we hit Memphis traffic.

"Elvis Presley Boulevard," she muses as we pass under that sign. "Good God."

"Not an Elvis fan?"

"You kidding? Elvis was the world's biggest perv. I read a book about him once. All he did was finger sixteen-year-old girls. He never fucked a grown woman in his life. And he wouldn't even fuck the little girls he fingered, because then he'd lose interest in them afterwards, so he just kept fingering them to death. Uh-oh. You're not going to shoot me with your gun for making fun of Elvis, are you?"

I shrug, wait a moment, then tell her, "I never used to like Elvis, either, until I went to Graceland."

"Ooh, you went to Graceland. What's *that* like?" But before I can reply, she says, "I wonder who molested more children, Michael or Elvis? I'd like to see that chart. Not a pie chart, either. Like one with a line of little kids instead of numbers. Probably Michael, I'm guessing. I mean, at least Elvis didn't build an entire amusement park around fingering kids."

Imagining that chart makes me forget what I was going to say. And suddenly I've got that Public Enemy song about Elvis mixed into the morass of Beethoven meets banjo boy. *Straight up racist.* Boing-boing-boing. *Simple and plain.* Da-da-da-dum. *Motherfuck him and John Wayne.*

"It's kinda like religion," I say.

"What is?"

"Graceland. Going to Graceland is. Like you start off as this atheist Elvis-hater in the whatever, the living room. Wall-to-wall cracker heaven, right? It's a fucking ranch house. Then you enter the gold-record room, and you're like *holy shit it's like nine million gold records in here!*—I didn't know there were that many destitute black song-writers in the Delta. Still trying to be cynical, you know? Then finally you enter the jumpsuit room and it's game over. You fall to your knees, and by the time you walk outside to the family gravesite by the cement pond you're devoted to Elvis forever."

"If you didn't like Elvis, why'd you go to Graceland? I mean, you don't like guns, and you got a gun. You don't like Elvis, and you go to Graceland. Are you some kind of masochist who likes being tied up and shit?"

I consider that.

"I don't think so. I mean, I've never tried it. It might be cool."

"Not me. I prefer the other end of the whip."

We get quiet for a minute as a series of images flutter through my brain like a flip-book in which I am tied to a bed being whipped by a gun-wielding stick-figure Samantha.

"I went to Graceland because I took my son there when he was recovering from a car accident. He had to wear a neck brace for three months and he stayed with me the whole time. I'd never seen anybody so miserable. But he loves music, so one day I took him to Graceland, and it was, I dunno, I'm sorry, but it was incredible. I'll always love Elvis for that day with my son—even if he did finger sixteen-year-old girls. Elvis is the fucking king." I take my foot off the accelerator and tell her, "I'm afraid I'm going to have to ask you to get out of my cab now."

I wait a second and add, "That was a joke."

"Oh. Good. I wasn't sure."

"Yeah, nobody in Vermont ever got my jokes, either. They take things literally up there. In Mississippi we say the opposite of what we mean."

She's about to disparage that custom, but then changes her mind—I can see the transition in her face—and instead she asks me about my son, about his accident, and I give her the brief rendition, which ends with the *Bad Motherfucker* wallet.

"So he recovered okay?"

"Yeah. He's fine. Good as new. He owns a record store now and kicks my ass in chess every day. It's funny—I mean, weird—I still hate getting beat by him in chess even though there was a time when I'd have cut off both my arms to lose a game of chess to him again."

"You'd have to move with your teeth."

"Huh?"

"Without any arms."

"Oh," I say, but I'm only pretending to understand.

"How long was your son in a coma?"

"Just a couple weeks. Nowhere near the family record."

"You have a family coma record?"

"Yeah. My mom owns the record at three and a half months. I mean, I guess she owns it. She died—I was eighteen—so maybe hers doesn't count. In which case my dad would own the record at three weeks for the first time he committed suicide."

"The first time?"

"Yeah. He botched it. With pills. Was in a coma for three weeks, came out of it, then signed one of those do-not-resuscitate contracts and did it again. That second time he went into another coma, for a month, but I guess that one doesn't count, either, because he died. I'm the only person in my family that's never been in a coma—knock on . . ."—I glance around the cab—" . . . Shakespeare," I say and thump his monstrous forehead with one knuckle and send him spinning.

"Dude, I don't know if I'd go knocking on Shakespeare for good luck. I mean, didn't he basically torture his characters to death?"

I ponder that. Yes, I decide, she's right. That's exactly what Shakespeare did. He created the most fascinating people on earth and then made them grovel for their deaths.

"Speaking of torture, how long were you married?"

"Huh?"

"How-long-were-you-married?"

"Oh. Just long enough to get talked into moving to Vermont. As soon as we got there she divorced me, and after that I was stuck in this blizzard that lasted eighteen years. That seasonal depression shit, it doesn't play around. By May every year I'd be walking through the woods and all I'd do—I couldn't stop doing this—I'd start picking out good trees to hang myself from. That was my relationship with nature."

"Hey, I got an idea. Why come you don't use that gun of yours to kill my husband? Then we could both be rich. We could live in Mexico. Or Hawaii."

I think that over.

"That's probably not a good idea, either."

I'm turning my attention back to the road when I hear a voice inside my head. It's a new voice, Eastwood-esque, and it says three words and stops and doesn't say anything else.

"I'm Black Magic," I repeat.

"What?"

"Nothing. I think I just named my gun."

"Black Magic? *That's* what you're naming it?"

"Yeah, that's its name."

She mulls this over.

"It's kinda a spooky name, for a gun, if you ask me. But the important thing is that you like it." A minute later, she adds, "It'd be a better name for a horse than a gun."

It's dusk when we get off at the hotel exit and park under the awning outside the Marriott.

"Still nothing," she says and shrugs.

I have all her stuff locked in my trunk. This is understood between us as I kill the engine and an almost audible awkwardness descends upon the cab. We open our doors when the air-conditioning wears off and steal glances at each other.

Suddenly my phone rings.

"Hon?" she says. "He's got a gun. Did I mention that he has a gun?" She listens for a minute, nods, and finally she wrinkles her nose and says, "Okay, baby. I know. This sucks. I'm sorry. Thank you. No, I wasn't making that up, he really does have a gun. It's named Black Magic. I offered him money to shoot you with it, but he wouldn't do it. He's like the last honest cabbie."

After hanging up she shrugs at me again. Like she has no idea about anything.

"He said he did it twenty minutes ago, that's all I know."

"Did what?"

"Transferred the money, idjut."

"Oh. Yeah."

We sit there waiting under the flickering blue neon. A grasshopper lands on the hood and makes me wonder if the old farmer I left in that trailer is a skeleton now. Was that yesterday or today? I can't decide. My life doesn't really feel divided into days and nights anymore. A different system of measurement has taken over, one partitioned by meals, nightmares, unexpected naps, smoke breaks, bowel movements, tantrums, and near-death experiences.

I start to tell Samantha I'm late to pick up somebody at the hospital, but I don't, and the reason I don't tell her this is because I'm half hoping she's going to invite me into her hotel room. I mean, if she does, I could call Stella and tell her the car broke down. Hell, I could just text her that and turn off my phone. It might be cool. Maybe it'd be like a sign, you know? One door closes, another opens. I'm thinking, yeah, a little whiskey and I might happily peel that tie-dye off Samantha. Maybe that's what I need. Yeah, maybe I need a California sex addict to tie me up and . . .

"It's here," she announces. "Presto chango."

She hands me her credit card. I insert the doohickey thing into my phone and run it. Then, after it's approved, I pop the trunk and set her garbage bags on the sidewalk.

"Boy, are they going to be impressed with me. Who's the redneck now, huh?"

"What about that bottle?"

"Oh, I've still got some beers left. Anyway, if I need more, there's a liquor store in walking distance—didn't you notice it?"

My disappointment is obvious. Picking up on that, she grins and sticks out her hand for me to shake and then jukes me out and pecks me on the cheek.

"Thanks for not dispersing me," she says.

And that's that. My beautiful sex-addict girlfriend whom I might have loved forever is gone, and I am once again driving alone through oblivion.

# BLACK MAGIC

Speaking to you as an escaped Vermonter who survived seventeen and a half suicidal winters in ski country, I can say with some confidence that life on earth is some serious Black Diamond bullshit. If we are down here on this planet by choice—something I seriously doubt—then we are very brave creatures, every one of us, even those assholes who wear sunglasses backward on their necks. Because life on this planet is hard, y'all. You can literally get eaten alive down here by all sorts of monsters, by crocodiles, tigers, sharks, psycho-killers, gangrene, fire ants, or piranha. But the worst monster of them all, the one that will fuck you up worse than a hundred hungry cheetahs, is the automobile wreck, that ultimate predator who can spit you out through broken glass or masticate your limbs with jagged metal. Getting eaten by a car wreck is the one way you most don't want to die on earth, and yet it never stops happening, a new sacrifice every second. It's such a horrific lottery to consider that we won't even let ourselves think about that monster at all—but it's there, it's there, we all know it's there . . .

Memphis traffic is wound tight, and I'm traveling in somnambu-
lant circles, weaving in and out of lanes, trying to find this organ-swap
hospital on the GPS. Ever visited Memphis? It's a charming city aside
from the parts that were bombed during World War II. Another interesting thing about Memphis is the proximity of great wealth to dire
poverty, which keeps everybody on their toes. It's dusk now, the
gloaming, and I can't find the hospital and finally conclude it must be
some wing of the main hospital. I park out front and call this guy
David to let him know I'm outside. Coughing through a feeble voice,
he tells me he'll be down shortly.

"I'm not moving too quick these days," he adds before hanging up
mid-cough.

Not liking the sound of that, I settle in to wait. I assume my fare
to be discharging with some new organ nestled inside his body. I'm
sure I'll hear all about his operation in excruciating detail as soon as
he plops into my cab.

While waiting I pick up my paperback. Samantha moved the
bookmark so I start reading where she left it except I have to keep
clench-blinking my eyes to stop the letters from climbing my hands
like fleas. The book is making the argument that the experience
called enlightenment, that flood of indescribable knowledge where
you become one with the universe, was a concept taken from the
Hindu Upanishads, which, over time, got layered over the Buddha's
forest teachings. But this guy Gotama, my book argues, disdained all
things metaphysical, esoteric, reincarnative, and championed not
enlightenment but a simple state of peace that arrived naturally after
you abandoned the habit of conceptual thinking. The book also
made it clear that Gotama's path had nothing to do with purity,
which was another Hindu concept. All Gotama taught, it said, was a

technique, the world's most logical way to reset your thought patterns in order to make you incredibly mellow and super chill, like Mr. Spock after *pon farr*.

Gotama was like the Opposite Buddha, is what I'm thinking, and I'm trying to make sense of that riddle and decide if this particular insight is going to stop me from raining down curses on old ladies in Sunday traffic. *Peace*, I keep thinking. Yeah, I'll take some of that. *Peace, peace, peace*, I start repeating in my lagging head until my one open eye spots this cadaverous white guy shaped like a bowling ball waddling out of the hospital pulling a suitcase on rollers like it's an obstinate dog. I know instantly he's my fare, my fate. He's supposed to be in a wheelchair, right? And where's his discharge orderly? No, something's afoot here. I don't even want to get out of the cab to help this guy. Please don't make me. Just let me sit here, okay?

When he raps on my window, I hide the book under my seat next to the gun and get outside the cab to wrestle him inside. He wants to sit up front, of course, and so I sprawl him facedown on the bench seat and situate his legs forward—butt-crack city—before raising his glob-layered torso and buckling in his lard belly. The smell of shat bananas pervades the Town Car. He's wheezing between death rattles and trying to light a cigarette with a shaky hand.

After putting his suitcase in the trunk I get behind the wheel. He's still trying to light the cigarette. I switch on *Commodores Live!* but as soon as the music starts I zone out and suddenly I'm back in ninth grade dipping Skoal during a bomb threat.

"Are we going to sit here all night?" David asks.

I startle awake—wow—then look over at him.

"No smoking," I say.

He takes the cigarette out of his mouth to stare at it, as if it had spoken to him and not me. His hand keeps trembling like in a cartoon electrocution.

"Stella always lets me smoke."

"Do I look like Stella?"

He takes another drag of the trembling cigarette, coughs a while, then asks, "Can we at least lose the jungle music?"

I don't respond other than to stare a warning at the cigarette. Then something horrible happens. At that moment, right as I'm about to threaten him, David turns his face toward me for the first time and we make unavoidable eye contact and suddenly I am very afraid. Holy fuck! It's his eyes, man. His eyes are bright yellow. The whites of his eyes, I mean. They aren't white. They are demonic glow-in-the-dark yellow.

"What's wrong with you?" I demand. "Why wasn't there an orderly with you?—why weren't you in a . . . wheelchair thing?"

The radioactive eyes above his plumb-tipped nose continue to wound my soul until I look away. As I do this, I am trying to deduce what organ has been replaced inside his body. Good God, did they give him the eyes of an executed murderer? Did they pop in some kind of nocturnal baboon eyes? What the fuck is wrong with this guy?

"Can you please get us out of here before they come chasing after me?"

"Chasing?" I mutter.

"Yeah. I was scheduled for surgery but fuck it my room was too cold. The bitch nurse wouldn't turn up the heat. Let's get a move on, huh? Hey, you mind stopping at a store. God—what's that smell?"

I test the air.

"Teddy," I reply after a moment.

He takes another puff and flicks the cigarette out the window. It almost hits an old man on the sidewalk.

"Happy now?" he asks.

I hesitate only a moment before pulling away from the hospital. There's a convenience store around the corner. I park there, and for a moment we are both quiet.

"I guess you want me to go in there for you, huh?"

He says yes, he'd appreciate that, then asks me to buy him a six-pack of beer, whatever's on sale. "If Coors Light is on sale get that."

I tell him he can't drink beer in my cab. "I'll lose my job if we get pulled over." Usually I could give a fuck if someone drinks, but I have the feeling this guy is going to croak at any moment, which in turn will kill me. They'll find both of us dead at the WELCOME TO MISSISSIPPI rest stop. No one will understand how it happened.

After I tell him I won't get him any beer, he glares at me with those toxic eyes until I look away again. Liver? Is that it? He was supposed to get a new liver? But then his hospital room got too cold so he . . . called a cab? I wonder if I'm breaking any laws. Am I an accomplice again? Am I aiding and abetting a suicide by cab?

"Mister, are you sure we shouldn't go back? I won't charge you anything. You don't look so hot."

"Just get me some water, okay? Like a really big bottle. And can you turn on the heat please?"

"The heat? You want me to turn on the heat?"

"Please. I'm freezing here."

I turn on the heater even though it's eighty degrees outside and go buy him some water. As I wait in line I look through the plate glass at the sunken Town Car, a travesty of a cab. It'll be parked in a junkyard soon, a fact that makes me inordinately sad. Outside again, I walk around the cab examining each threadbare tire. I open the trunk and try flipping the switch again, but the air shocks only sigh. Finally I get back inside and open the bottle of water and hand it to him. I do all this petulantly, letting him know he's a pain in the ass. Then, just before I merge back into traffic, I recall what the Buddha said about conceptual thinking, about avoiding attraction and aversion, and then I think about what Bill Hicks said about another choice we always have, the choice between fear and love. *The eyes of fear want you to put bigger locks on your doors, buy guns, close yourself off. The eyes of love, instead, see all of us as one.* I stop the cab at the edge of the parking lot under a red neon Budweiser sign and turn to the almost dead man beside me. It feels as if I am holding a loaded gun to my own head in order to be nice to him.

"What kind of music you like?" I ask.

Like a quick left jab, this catches him off guard, the kindness does.

"What?" he snaps.

I adjust my tone, soften it, and ask him again what kind of music he likes.

"I like country," he replies cautiously.

"Country," I repeat. "Okay."

I try to visualize the stash of CDs in my trunk zipped inside the small travel bag.

"Skynyrd or Old 97's?" I ask him. "That's all the country I got."

"Skynyrd," he says and begins coughing again.

I get outside and walk around to the back of the car. Inside the trunk is a ten-CD console set beside the metal box that records the movie of my life. I remove the Commodores and stare at the disk, tilting it this way and that to increase its iridescence. After another spell of lost time, I insert the Skynyrd CD and get back inside the cab.

It's twilight as I pull away from the convenience store with Dead David in tow. Even though I've made this trip a hundred times I get trapped in the wrong lane and we lose ten minutes and end up exiting the city via Highway 278, a route I usually avoid after dark because of the deer. David is pissed at my mistake. When he says, "Maybe I should drive?" I take my foot off the accelerator and say, "Or maybe I should take you back to the hospital where you belong?"

Our eyes meet again. For a moment I enter a jaundiced abyss of fear and hate that makes my own abyss of fear and hate look like a cruise ship.

"Okay, you win. I'm sorry. Take me home, please."

I push the accelerator and off we go.

"You know Kirby?" he asks a few miles later.

"Kirby?" I reply, my voice thick with distaste. "Yeah, I know Kirby. He works nights so I don't see him much anymore."

"You don't work nights?"

"No. I used to. But I kept getting in fights with drunk frat boys."

"Kirby always lets me drink in his cab."

"I'm not Kirby," I whisper.

Quiet.

"Sorry. It's just that I've really been looking forward to that beer. Not to mention a smoke."

"You'll be home soon."

"Not at the rate we're moving."

We drive the next fifteen minutes in silence. I'm sipping my Red Bull to stay awake. Meanwhile the heat inside the cab ignites the tang of urine. My head starts to swim until I remember to follow my breath again. Then I fall asleep for a moment and have to jack-knife back onto the interstate. David doesn't say anything right away. He's eager to say something, but has thought better of it. Finally he can't contain himself any longer and turns to me, his yellow eyes lasering into mine, and mutters, "Lemme know if you're gonna do that again, huh?"

I laugh in spite of myself and once again begin to feel badly about how I'm treating David. After all, he'll probably be dead by Holly Springs. Would it kill me to be nice to him during his final few miles of life? Why is kindness so motherfucking hard?

"Sorry, man," I manage to say. "It's been a long damn day."

"Oh. You think you've had a long day, huh?"

I don't reply to that, although it gives me something to consider. Samantha said the same thing, right? Or was it Abigail said it? I'm still pondering this, mulling the likelihood that somebody on earth—maybe millions of people on earth—are currently having worse days than I am having. Is that possible? If so, what the fuck is wrong with this planet? Meanwhile a part of my brain is still screaming *Stella gutted Tony's dad!* Another part is tied to a bed making love to Samantha in the Marriott. And a smaller lobe is worrying about Althea and the old farmer and wondering where will Miko live?

"Go ahead and light up," I tell David. "Long as you roll down your window."

He lights a shuddering cigarette and rolls down the window about an inch. The air rushing into the cab at least clears out the smell of urine. He's smoking cross-armed, because he's freezing now. Halfway through the cig he starts coughing and then throws it outside and rolls up the window like he just survived a Vermont blizzard.

"They gave me the wrong colored jello," he tells me a few minutes later.

The heat is making me dizzy, and at first I assume I've heard him wrong.

"I don't like the green."

"That's why you left the hospital?"

He takes another sip of water and sneers snobbishly at the label.

"No, not exactly. I buzzed the nurse—she hates me—we got into another argument about, you know, the shitty food. Then I asked her to turn up the heat—she wouldn't—so I called Stella and told her to send a cab. Stella always lets me drink beer."

I smile in the dark and remain quiet.

"What's wrong with this car anyway? It feels like we're midgets."

"It's had a long day too."

We drive in silence another five miles and then he points his shivering finger at my flying-saucer air freshener and asks, "You believe in those things?"

I don't reply at first because it's a complicated subject with me and I'm tired, but at the same time I'm aware that my silence feels belligerent. I keep reminding myself this guy is suffering horribly. I want to be kind to him but it feels so impossible. We remain quiet while listening to "Tuesday's Gone," which gets me thinking about the end of *Dazed and Confused*, the part where the keg runs dry. We're about ten miles from our exit onto the deer-haunted two-lane that will wind us through the night into Gentry, just me and this guy with glow-in-the-dark eyes who will be dead on arrival.

The stars are coming out by the time I answer David's question about flying saucers. Everybody asks about the Bigfoot air freshener, but nobody asks about the flying saucer, not until today—and today

I've been asked what . . . two, three times? It must be a sign. What the fuck? I mean, what does it matter if this asshole thinks I'm nuts? He'll be dead soon anyway.

So I point to the saucer air freshener and tell him, "One night I picked up my friend Vance and his head cook, this guy Nat, at the airport back in Memphis. They'd both been on vacation. At the airport I gave Vance the wheel and we're heading back home—in fact, we're right about here on the interstate. It's dark out, like now, and suddenly Vance points ahead of us up the highway, to those trees, and says, *What the hell is that?*"

For emphasis I point ahead of us and repeat, "What the hell is that?"

David stares at my finger like a jaundiced dog.

"I look up and sure enough there's this light thing hovering above the trees on the left side of the interstate—this really bright white light—but it's like a mile away and I figure it's some kind of radio tower thing, right? 'I've been watching that light for ten minutes,' Vance says, 'but we aren't getting any closer to it.' And I start paying attention to the light. After all, Vance is a down-to-earth guy, and I'm the one who's always babbling about Pascagoula flying saucers and anal-probe robots, so, whatever, I start watching the light, and, yeah, it is weird—it's not a normal light at all. At first, it's like Vance said, we're not getting any closer to it, but what's even weirder is the light itself, it keeps changing shape, like the light doesn't radiate outward, it's like . . . contained, like a bag of light. One minute it looks like an armadillo and the next it looks like a deer, it keeps changing shape, and we keep driving along for another few minutes watching it until we're about two miles from the exit—right about where we are now— when suddenly the light starts moving over those trees toward us.

Holy shit, you know? It's still to the left of the interstate but now it's suddenly getting bigger and bigger."

I pause in case he wants to shut me up, but to my surprise he doesn't say anything sarcastic, so I raise my arm and point ahead again.

"It's right over there now, man. And we're trying to make sense of it, you know? It seems impossible it could be a plane—no way—so the only reasonable explanation is a helicopter pointing a spotlight at us, right? Wrong. It keeps getting closer and I'm starting to get that famil-iar feeling. I'm in the passenger seat holding a quart of Bud while this bag of white light keeps closing in on us. What the fuck is it? Fuck! I dunno what it is, man, but it's coming right at us, it's getting really close. We're taking turns saying, *what the fuck is that?* We keep saying it louder and louder until we're like, WHAT THE FUCK IS THAT? It's moving toward the highway now and coming right at us and get-ting wide as the windshield. There's no sound I can hear, but, hell, we're in a Lexus doing sixty. Actually we're moving a lot slower now because Vance is freaked out. I'm just glad he didn't blink his head-lights at it. Trust me, I've read a lot about this type shit. Never blink your lights at a UFO."

Again I pause to allow David to make fun of me. Yet he remains oddly silent, his jaundiced eyes staring blankly ahead as if watching the UFO move toward us.

"So this blob-of-light thing—here it comes, man—like it's timing itself to cross the highway directly over our heads. Vance and I are both leaning forward to watch it through the windshield. And that's when I notice this blue light thing, like a blue orb, drop off the edge of this blob of white light and descend into the trees. I'm like, 'dude, you see that?' Then I see another orb drop and I point and yell, 'There's another one!'"

I thump the flying-saucer air freshener with my bird finger.

"Then, right before it crosses the highway over us, I tell Vance to open the sunroof and I stand up on the seat and stick my body outside into the wind, which gives me this incredible view of . . . whatever it is, this blob of weird light crossing the highway above us on a clear night, lots of stars out. It's so close I could've hit it with a slingshot. And when it gets almost directly over the car—boom—its base suddenly becomes visible to us. It's like this perfect triangle craft with a circular white light on each point—with the bag-of-light thing radiating out of the top of the triangle. The base isn't that big—you could have landed it in a baseball infield—and the very center of it contains these grayish metal cylinders. Other than those cartridges, the whole triangular craft seems to emit light, like a fabric of light, like fluorescent tubing does. It's a light ship, man. That's the only way I can describe it, a fucking light ship. And it's beautiful. So there I am standing above the car holding a quart of Bud and staring up into this light ship and grinning and waving at it. I'm not scared for once in my life. I'm like *welcome to earth, bitches.* It's weird how happy I am as it passes right over the car and I'm waving up at it like some idiot redneck in a Budweiser commercial—*this Bud's for you!*—and at the same time I'm kinda seeing how stupid I must look to the aliens or whatever inside it. It passes right over us until it's on the right side of the interstate, like it just took the off-ramp into Holly Springs—the one right here—and that's when something crazy happens. What it did next seems impossible. Like . . . rolling in place, except the center of the craft, the cartridge compartment, stayed in one place. I swear to God it felt like it was showing off. You know, doing tricks to freak me out. Nobody saw this part except me because I'm still up in the sunroof. Meanwhile this thing is fucking shape-shifting and shit, and

I'm shouting down to Vance and Nat what I'm watching. At first I thought it was rotating around the axis of the cartridges so that the bottom of the craft became the top of the craft, but it was more complicated than that, more magical, more . . . Japanese. And right as this is happening, Vance veers off the highway after it. He hits the exit ramp so fast I bang my ribs into the sunroof and squat back into the car while Vance keeps following the UFO to that Walmart right over there. See that gas station? Wait, I'll show you. Here's where we finally stopped chasing it."

I stop near the gas station at the edge of the Walmart parking lot. The main building complex, which is lit up with yellow lights—the same diseased color as David's eyes—resembles an eerie outpost on Mars.

"That's where it stopped, right behind the main building over that field. We could still see its lights, but we couldn't figure out how to get any closer to it. We watched it for another ten minutes—it just sat there—then finally we're like *well, fuck it, let's go home*. So we did—after checking to make sure it wasn't five hours later, right? And the whole drive back we keep looking for it, like expecting it to drop down in front of us like a giant spider. But it didn't come back. Probably because we never blinked our headlights at it."

It occurs to me that David hasn't spoken for a long time. The two of us sit there in silence staring at Walmart. I'm starting to get that spooky feeling. Like maybe I've summoned the aliens by telling that story about them. I get all tingly and déjà vu-ey.

"Tell you the truth, man," I whisper after a moment, "that's not the first one I've seen. I'm like the UFO whisperer or something—I've been seeing 'em my whole life—I don't know why—maybe because I've been looking for them all my life. And it's always when I'm in cars, and it's always those triangle ones."

Then I start telling him about the other times I've seen them. By now I'm starting to worry that I'm babbling to a corpse. Part of the reason I keep talking to David is to avoid acknowledging that he's dead. Eventually I shut up. I'm still staring at that spot behind Walmart where the light ship hovered that night. Then I start thinking about Mayfern and wondering if maybe she was inside the UFO. Was hers a saucer or a triangle one? We sit there in silence another minute, just me and Dead David, until he asks, "Are you drunk? Are you on drugs right now? Seriously, am I even safe driving with you? Why the hell are we stopped here?"

It's such a relief he's not dead. Like all of a sudden I'm so grateful to him for not being dead. Without answering him, I get out of the taxi and walk across the lot into the gas station and a few minutes later come outside with a Bud tallboy and hand it to him.

"Merry Christmas," I say.

After we pull onto the two-lane, David clears his throat and says thanks before belching. Again we get quiet—except for his burping—he's burping a lot—and now I'm starting to worry about my driving. I'm light-headed from the heat—meanwhile he's trembling cold—and suddenly I don't feel at all steady behind the wheel. It's possible I've had too much Red Bull, like maybe I've ODed on it.

"So you were at the hospital to get some kind of organ thing?" I ask, trying to keep myself alert.

He burps again and says, "Liver."

"Ah," I say.

A mile passes before I ask how long he had to wait before a liver came up for sale.

"Four months. They told me if it'd been five I'd be dead."

That gives me something to fixate on besides my obsession with deer. Whenever I study the shoulder of the road I'm seeing entire herds of them. Not that they're real—at least I'm pretty sure they're not real—but I see them every time I look, their eyes glowing red along the roadside like malevolent hitchhikers. "You are not real," I keep telling myself, "you're like roadkill ghosts or something."

"What's not real?"

"Nothing. I didn't mean to say that out loud."

Now I feel stupid and the ensuing silence makes it worse. Plus I'm getting twitchy and starting to see other things besides deer. "Spooky out tonight," I whisper to break the spell. I wish I hadn't told him about all the UFOs I've seen. Telling those kind of stories is worse than blinking your headlights at them. I keep glancing into the sky, which causes me to swerve into those bumpy things that line the road. We drive another ten minutes in this fashion before David clears his throat and tells me he needs to pee. We are on an empty two-lane in the middle of nowhere, it's night, it's like a thousand degrees inside the Town Car, and now the dead guy next to me needs to pee—something I'm pretty sure he's going to need my help doing.

"Now? You have to pee now?"

"Right now. Pull over at the next dirt road, huh. Hurry. And can you turn that down, it's making it worse."

I turn down "Free Bird," which is on the soaring part, then pull onto a dirt road far enough in that a cop won't spot us. I stop the car and we wait there idling while staring through the windshield at all the stars. I'm afraid to leave the cab. I can feel them out there watching us. David shifts around until it becomes clear he can't even get out by himself. Finally, as if watching myself from above, I open the door and step onto the dirt road. With a wary glance into the woods,

I walk around the car while massaging my lower back and then wrangle David out of the cab and hold him upright beneath the armpits from behind while he fumbles with his fly beneath a million stars. He pees for a really long time—it's a weak yet persistent stream that's going all over his pant legs and tennis shoes—and I'm trying to increase its arc by leaning him backward when something inside my spine goes *ping-ping-ping*—a bit of déjà vu here—and then there's this electrical agony. The only way to stop the spasming is to collapse like a house of cards, which is what I do while the world holds its belly and chuckles. Yeah, the old back spasm joke never gets old. There's some consolation in the fact David doesn't fall backward and crush me, though certainly the gods of karma missed an opportunity there. When the spasms become less excruciating, I turn my head, resting my cheek on the dirt road, to establish that David has made it back into the car and closed the door. The headlights are shining ahead of us down the dirt road, where I can make out a strange apelike figure moving long-armed in the distance. When I look toward my feet, I realize I am lying on a slope about three feet downstream from David's pee puddle. An estuary of glistening pee is crawling between my legs toward my scrotum.

"You okay?" David rolls down his window to ask.

"Yeah, fantastic," I reply while the pee snake slithers toward my crotch.

"What's wrong with you?"

At first I don't understand that it's a question and not an insult.

"Back spasms. I'll be okay as long as I don't move."

I try to wriggle away from his pee, but the spasms return in all their agony and then I feel his wetness seeping into my crotch. Pressing my back into the dirt road to stop the spasms, I stare straight up as a glowing saucer traverses the sky. Finally, a saucer! It hovers above the Town Car and keeps disappearing and then reappearing in a different spot. Then there's another saucer, and another. Soon the sky is crowded with an apocalypse of saucers. As long as I stare at them it feels as if I'm being pleasantly electrocuted. But when I close my eyes it stops.

David yells out the window, "Hey, is that Shakespeare?"

The question confuses me and I glance toward the woods, where I spot a bonfire burning behind the trees surrounded by dark figures cloaked in red djellabas. I can hear gurgled words like a spell of glossolalia. Is it Jason out there? Are the woods filled with Satanists? David yells something else out the window, but I'm too busy trying to worm my body away from his electric pee snake to understand him. Gravel digs into my spine.

"While we're young," he shouts a moment later.

I start to curse his mother in Spanish but then remember the car is running and that he could shimmy behind the wheel and leave me at this crossroads to be sacrificed by Satanists or probed by aliens or gangbanged by malicious deer. Everywhere I look I see a host of red eyes feasting on me. The ghosts of murdered Indians lurk behind trees. Then I notice the front passenger tire is dangerously low.

Eventually I roll over and start crawling on hands and knees toward the cab. Thank God I left the door open. I grab at the steering wheel and use it to lift myself behind the wheel like someone without legs would. Then we've escaped and are back on the highway, but I'm still worried. I've never had the spasms attack me while I'm driving. I'm not sure how that would play out. Wondering, and imagining the worst, I take an Advil that has survived a wash cycle from my shirt pocket and swallow it with the spit dregs of the last motherfucking Red Bull I will ever drink in my life.

A few miles later David falls asleep. As soon as he starts snoring and I have no corroborating witness, all hell breaks loose. Witches riding three-legged deer stagger across the highway. Zeta Reticulans hitch-hiking with Elvis. An albino possum leaps onto the hood of the car and starts clawing at the windshield like it's trying to get inside. When I glance into the rearview, the whole team is back there: the old guy in the hospital gown, the Goth girl, the farmer, the screaming baby. Grasshoppers start landing in my hair, and I'm swatting them away and swerving wildly. William Faulkner is standing on the side of the highway holding a watermelon. As we pass him, our eyes meet, and he gives me the finger.

"You aren't really there," I keep thinking. "You motherfuckers are just in my mind."

"What?" David says. "Who the hell are you talking to now?"

"I was just singing along," I tell him and turn up the volume on "That Smell."

He falls back to sleep a minute later and I consider taking a pull from his Budweiser, but when I pick up the can, it's almost empty and no way am I drinking death's backwash. By now I'm sweating like crazy, and the urine smell is choking the oxygen from the air. I reach into the phone console to find my asthma inhaler and start puffing it. I can see the yellow glow of David's eyes burning behind his lids while he snores. Then, slowly, slowly, the glow subsides until it fades out entirely. A rictus smile overtakes his face, an evil clown emerging . . .

"Hey, mister, are you dead?" I shout.

I'm pretty sure the question saves his life. He sputters upward, reemerging from the underworld, and looks around like somebody's just robbed him. He even pats at his various pockets.

"What the hell?" he yells at me.

"We're almost there. Where do you live?"

He gives me an address not far from campus, an apartment complex called the Windsors.

"You know where that is?" he asks, and I say yeah I know where that is.

Then, just as we are taking the exit ramp, David tells me he can't find his credit card. I tighten my grip on the wheel as he continues to search his wallet.

"I must have left it on the hospital table after you made me read those numbers to you on the phone." He says this as if it's my fault he can't pay me. He looks through his wallet again and finally tosses it on the dash. "I guess I should call the hospital."

We're on Coleman Road, a steep decline into town that happens to go past the police station, which has an antique police car parked out front. We are not there yet, but I can already see the cherry on top.

"How are you going to pay me?"

"You take checks, right? Stella lets me pay with checks."

"We don't take checks. That's why I called you. To make sure you weren't going to pay me with a damn check."

I take a hard right into the police station and find a slot facing the brick building.

"Keep looking," I say.

"Don't you have the numbers writ down?"

"No. I was driving and couldn't write them down."

"Then why'd you make me read them to you?"

"Because people without credit cards don't know how many numbers to make up."

"Oh. Well, shit, all I got's this check I can sign over to you. It's that or nothing."

"You know where we are, right?"

He looks up at the building but seems confused, lost.

"What kind of car is that over there?" I ask.

We both stare at the antique cop car. I'm worried that if the cops come out they'll arrest me. There's an open container in the cupholder and a gun under my seat that has probably murdered thousands of people. A glance in the rearview confirms that I look like an escaped convict with a trunk full of bodies. I need to get out of here, I realize. This was a terrible mistake. A cop could come out at any moment and shoot me dead and they'd give him a medal.

David shows me a check made out to somebody else. It's for $120 and has already been signed over once.

"You can't sign over checks twice," I say.

"Sure you can. I do it all the time."

"What do you mean you do it all the time?"

"It's a hundred and twenty. That's what I owe you, right?"

"First off, you owe me one fifty. And I already told you we don't take checks. We take cash or cards. You want me to drive you by an ATM?"

"Are you retarded? I just told you I can't find my card."

"Maybe you need to look harder. Or maybe I should go fetch a cop to help you look."

I'm bluffing here. The only way I'm going into that police station is in handcuffs.

A minute later he says, "Here it is. Whew."

"Yeah, whew."

I insert the doohickey thing into my phone and run the card and then hand him my phone and watch as he skips the tip page. My crotch is soaked with his urine yet he is stiffing me. I think about the gun under my seat and imagine placing it to his temple.

"Just sign with your finger," I tell him.

He does. And much to my surprise the card is accepted.

That done, I drive him to the Windsors, which is a downtrodden apartment complex that caters mostly to international students. After parking in front of his apartment I just sit there like *okay you no-tip son of a bitch get out of my cab and let's see who's retarded now huh motherfucker?* Then, suddenly, I recall this morning's resolution to be kinder to people. Who was that strange man wooing the dark? Fuck that guy, I decide.

"Don't forget your bag," I say cruelly and pop the trunk.

"Can you lend me a hand, please?"

"Crawl on your own, buddy. I did."

As we wait each other out, two couples walk by with some kids between them and they all turn to stare at the Town Car, which appears to be sinking back-end first into some tar pit of time. A portrait in decrepitude, David begins to warple and shimmy his way out of the sedan, a task made only slightly less painful by its close proximity to the ground. Grappling against the roof, he sidles his way toward the trunk while I watch his hobbling progress with a Zen-like ambivalence. "There is no God judging me," I remind myself while letting David struggle with his suitcase, but eventually I sigh and open my door and get his bag out for him and wheel it to the front door of his apartment only to turn around and find him seated back inside the cab dying of an asthma attack.

I limp over to his open door. Then I reach across him into the console and hand him my inhaler and watch as he hits it five times in a row. He doesn't return it.

"Let's go, big guy," I say, which is something I've always despised other men for saying. "We're going to take this really slow, okay?"

The first time I attempt to heft him out of the car everything goes wrong and we abort and I have to lie down on the pavement to rest my back. The second time I manage to get him to his feet. He clamps his arm around my titanium wing. I will not bore you here with more descriptions of pain. I ask him if he's ready and after a moment he says, "We'll find out."

"Left foot first," I say, and we take one step. Then another. Five minutes later we achieve the front door, where he begins fumbling after his key. When he pushes the door open, the first thing I notice, after the wave of ammonia rushes past us, is that he's a hoarder. Newspapers are piled to the ceiling. Magazines and paperbacks are stacked against every wall so that the living room to our left has been reduced to an igloo-sized compartment. The hallway in front of us has been similarly narrowed by books and dead-ends into a doorless bathroom filled with dozens of cats peering out at us. I stand there staring into this labyrinth of books. And they're not just any books. They're good books. For instance, I notice a Doctorow first edition. And, fuck, there's a stack of hardback Shakespeare on a wooden desk supporting a blue litter box and a green electric typewriter. There's even a sheet of paper in the typewriter. Oh my God is that a half-written poem? Have I driven into the future of my own death?

Suddenly I get this cold feeling in my testicles, like with wet swim trunks, and my head begins to throb in giant heartbeats. It's got to be a stroke. When I open my eyes again, twenty cats are staring at me from inside the hallway.

"Poor things," David says. "They haven't been fed in a week. That's the real reason I left."

"Reason what?" I ask after another spell of dizziness passes.

"The reason I left the hospital. The surgery kept getting delayed—the guy with the liver wouldn't fucking die already—and the guy who was feeding my cats had to leave town, and I knew they were starving to death."

"You—you . . . oh Jesus, where's their food at?"

After he tells me, I prop him against the wall and enter the maze of books to feed the hundreds of cats haunting his hoarder kitchen. I step in cat shit. I puddle through their urine. The cats are weaving through my legs trying to trip me up while purring and meowing ecstatically. When I reemerge from the kitchen, David is still leaning against the hallway wall. He opens his eyes very slowly and without malice until he sees me.

"Here," he says, handing me my inhaler.

"Keep it. I got another one at home."

"Take it. If it's yours I don't want it."

I take it and start to put my arm around his shoulders but he shirks me off.

"I don't need your goddamn help."

Then, talking to his cats in an Irish brogue, calling them *lads*, he begins waddling down the maze that ends in some hellish bed swamped with feces.

Alone again, I stand in the doorway a few seconds and then start hobbling toward my car, but at that moment an invisible cop steps out of a hedge and starts tasing my back until I collapse onto the sidewalk and flop around there for a few minutes. After the spasms taper off, I begin to feel extremely peaceful and am about to fall asleep on the sidewalk when five Indian women walk over to stare down at me in *Straight Outta Compton* style.

One of them asks if I'm okay, her voice void of compassion.

"Yeah. It's just . . . back spasms. Hey, do y'all know the guy that lives here? David?"

There's only one woman staring down at me now. I don't know what happened to the other four—maybe I imagined them? Maybe I'm suffering from stroke-induced fly eye? The one Indian woman staring at me is mid-fifties, her graying black hair pulled away from a discerning face.

"Is he drunk again?" she asks.

"No. I just picked him up from the . . . the hospital. He didn't have the . . . his surgery. He was supposed to get a . . . liver?—but he needed to . . . feed his . . . I think he's dying."

"Liver? Well, that figures."

"Listen. I'm afraid that if he dies . . . his cats might . . . you know . . . eat him."

She says something I can't understand and adds, "I've got his son's number somewhere. They hate each other. Do you think I should call him?"

"They hate each other?" I say, distraught.

She nods at me.

"God yes. Please call his son. Tell him the goddamn cats are eating his father."

"Okay. Calm down. I will. Did you go inside there?"

"Yeah."

"Did you happen to notice a black cat with one big white spot here who looks kind of like the whale in *Finding Nemo*?"

She points to her left eye as she says this. I'm pretty confused by her description.

"I can't remember."

"I think he stole my daughter's cat. You sure you're okay?"

"Yeah. I'll be gone in five minutes, I promise."

She leaves her patch of sky, and for a minute or an hour I stare into outer space, the stars floating around like dust motes. Eventually I roll over on the sidewalk and crawl hands-and-knees to the Town Car. While climbing in I notice a hundred-dollar bill on my floorboard. I don't dare reach for it but just sit there trying to figure out where it came from. Suddenly I realize it's Teddy's tip. Yeah, Tiff didn't rip me off after all. The C-note must have fallen there while she was molesting me. And I was going to murder them. I was going to fill Teddy's swimming pool with blood and write enigmatic song lyrics on the walls with their severed limbs. Jesus God, David left the hospital to feed his cats. Tony loves Cheryl more than I've loved anybody except maybe Davy Jones. Zeke plays catch with his daughter. Tiff's a brave defender of abused women. Is there not one person on earth I am better than? Is everyone but me a secret saint?

I turn off Skynyrd, flick on the AC, and aim for home.

At that moment Horace texts me a dispatch.

"Reb motel," it says.

How did he know?

"Off," I text back.

"Kirby sick. Backed up 6."

He's lying. Nobody backed up six rides would be sending coherent text messages. No, he's parked somewhere in a lap dance of pork ribs, the bastard. I don't respond to the text, but since I have to drive past the motel anyway I slow down as I approach the Rebel. Noticing the art hop is in progress, I pull into the lot and park far away from the festivities. I know that antagonizing Horace will make my life miserable—he wins all our petty battles—so I text him that I'm at the motel.

"Last one," I add.

I can barely keep my eyes open.

Two minutes later Horace replies, "Canceled. go campus condo bld 4."

I don't have the energy to flip him off. All I can do is sigh. I am the Beethoven of sighing.

"No mas," I text him back and then turn off my phone.

But I don't leave yet. I'm idling near the dark wing of the motel that's not being used for the art hop. There are hundreds of dead bugs splattered across my windshield. I try the wipers, but they just smear the carnage. Through the passenger window I can see my friend Jean Paul playing his guitar over by the Coke machine—a small crowd is gathered around him. Hipsters and bohèmes are migrating about. The meth-head twins are smoking cigs with Cancer Max near the ice machine. There's a tent set up with a garbage-barrel keg and lots of people are holding red plastic cups as they wander through the rooms filled with art. Tony is nowhere to be seen. Maybe he's standing in weeds holding his thumb out to headlights or maybe he's still asleep in his room dreaming about Cheryl. I look around for Moondog. I don't see him, although I do spot a woman holding the painting I wanted, the one of the Disco Limo. Hopefully nobody will buy his Town Car one. Maybe I can work out a payment plan with him later.

For a long time I sit there watching through the tinted window as Jean Paul strangles his guitar neck. Punk rock ages you fast, but he still has that voice, like scratching a blackboard. Jean Paul used to be my neighbor until his asshole landlord hiked his rent and he had to move ten miles outside of town, like most every artist in Gentry. The song he's strangling to death is the punk version of "Seasons in the Sun" that he stole from the band Too Much Joy. It's become Jean Paul's signature song, the one all his friends yell for him to play, his "Freebird." I roll down the passenger window to hear it better, but the window stops going down after one inch and makes a grinding noise instead. It won't go back up, either. Shit. Now none of the windows work. I sit there, half asleep, while Jean Paul screams as if in great pain, like a heathen being burned at the stake: "BUT THE STARS WE-COULD-REACH WERE JUST STARFISH-ON-THE-BEACH!"

Starfish, man . . . Hawaii . . . first memories, that moment it all starts, how you suddenly inhabit yourself without hope of escape, the body you're born with, the mind you get. When I wake up again, Jean Paul has quit playing, but folks are still wandering around checking out the art. I mop the drool off my face with my sleeve and am about to put the car into reverse—everything I do feels Herculean—when I recall that I can't go home, that Miko is there, and that I'll have to sleep on Vance's couch like I said I would. If I do go home, it might be years before I can break up with Miko again. But I don't want to sleep on Vance's couch. His dog Archie will hump my leg. My asthma will flare up. Oh, Miko, what should I do?

As if answering this question for me, the Town Car starts revving its engine—something to do with the timing mechanism. Either that or it's gone Killdozer on me. I've still got my hand on the gearshift but just stare out through the splattered bugs wondering what does it all mean? I keep watching everybody going room to room in search of art and beauty or maybe just trying to meet somebody and fall in love or at least get laid. In a town this size you know everyone, or it feels that way, and you also know the rumors and trysts and disgraces attached to each person. You know their most whispered-about moments. You know about her ménage à trois or the time he got caught spying through that bedroom window or the dog she kicked in the eye with her stiletto or the time he called a jazz musician that name and tried to steal his saxophone or how she got a DUI with her kids in the car or what he said about you behind your back. Everybody elicits a response, an emotion, be it lust, hate, fear, envy, admiration, even love. Staring out that buggy windshield, I sit there painting everybody with my misconceptions about them. None of it's true, not really. Or even if that rumor is true, you still don't know but a fraction of the story. You weren't there. You don't know that chick. You don't know that dude. Not really. Hell, you barely know yourself.

I fall back to sleep with my forehead wilted onto the steering wheel and then bolt awake scared as hell, not sure where I am or even who I am. The art hop has ended, and the idling Town Car is on empty with the red warning light on but not yet blinking. Everything is dark and quiet at the motel. Finally I remember my name, my life, where I live, all that. It hits me in a wave of disgust, and I groan and resign myself to it and am about to drive my sorry ass home and sneak inside like a thief to sleep on my couch when I notice Tony standing in front of the Coke machine kicking it. Maybe that's what woke me up. I keep watching him kick the machine harder and harder—he's really kicking the shit out of it—and then, suddenly, as if issued from inside the Coke machine, I hear a scream followed by a gunshot.

A moment later the red door in front of my cab bursts open and a giant with an albino Mohawk starts carrying one of the meth-head twins toward the gray van parked beside me. At one point she almost escapes—I think it's the younger woman, the wife, not the mother— but he catches her by the ponytail and starts dragging her down the sidewalk in front of my cab, her backside scraping along the sidewalk, her legs kicking like crazy.

"They are not your people," I tell myself.

He slides open the van door and starts shoving her inside—this is happening less than six feet from my window—and he's about to slide-shut the door on one of her legs when out of nowhere Tony vaults across my hood, springs onto Jason's back, gets an arm around his neck, another around his forehead—I'm pretty sure that's called a *sleeper hold* in professional wrestling—and pulls Jason away from the van as they crash backward onto the hood of the cab, causing me to accidentally hit the wiper switch. As the wipers squeak back and forth, the two men keep wrestling on the hood—the sleeper hold is definitely not working—but to my shock Tony pulls away and lands a good left, then a hard right cross, but Jason is like water off a duck with that shit and spits blood and then buries a roundhouse wrist-deep into Tony's mouth. He picks him up off the ground and throws Tony back onto the car hood. Then he lifts a black motorcycle helmet over his head and starts smashing it down onto Tony's forehead over and over.

I'm pretty sure Tony is already dead by the time I lurch out of the cab holding the towel with the gun wrapped inside it. When I try to unravel it, the gun spills onto the parking lot and I scramble after it and trip to my knees. Jason, who has started gargling out some obscene Klingon-sounding language, is still bashing in Tony's skull as I pick up the gun in both hands and stand up to aim it at the side of Jason's head. I hesitate only a moment before pulling the trigger, but of course nothing happens, and while I'm trying to figure out how to undo the safety, Jason's mother emerges pap naked from the motel room holding what appears to be the exact same gun as mine—this confuses me for a moment—the two of us stare at each other like into a funhouse mirror—and then a deer leaps through the windshield of my belly.

As the gunshot echoes, I keel forward until my forehead hits the parking lot and then I writhe around before settling onto my back and losing consciousness. When I wake up, Cancer Max is smiling down at me—his face as big as a parade float—and I try to apologize to him about the pizza but my throat feels flooded and I can't breathe. Again the darkness closes on me, and when I reemerge the world is frantic with stuttering blue lights. I'm so disoriented I assume the lights are attached to some flying saucer that's abducting me. When the lights suddenly turn red, the aliens jump out and start cutting away my clothes. A minute later I levitate inside a tractor beam and there's this long wail-whoosh of a siren and the familiar rush of the driving motion I know so well. Something's being clamped over my face and my stomach is on fire and I keep sputtering *oh God oh God oh God* until everything fades and the next thing I know I'm being wheeled through the emergency room—I turn my head and catch sight of Miss Pamela asleep on the couch—then I fade out again— I'm listening to frogs and staring at this lake covered in white mist— and when I reawaken I know it's for the last time—I get what's happening here—I've seen this movie—and there's Chloe staring down at me with those giant brown eyes so big I want to float up inside them, and while lost in those eyes I have no choice but to tell her the truth. I push the oxygen mask away from my mouth.

"I'm dying," I whisper to her.

After I say this, Chloe's face becomes impossibly hard, almost unrecognizable behind a fierceness I've never seen hinted at before and she forces a smile down upon me—somebody squeezes my hand—it might be her—I hope it's her—and we're still moving forward, still in motion, as she replaces the mask over my mouth and tells me, "Not on my watch, Lou. Not on my watch."

# ACKNOWLEDGMENTS

TWENTY YEARS between books leaves too many people to thank. To those who supported early drafts of this book: Mary Miller, Dan Kirschen & Andrianna Yeatts at ICM, Tony Perez at Tin House, George Saunders, Chris Offutt, Carol Ann Fitzgerald, Sy Safransky, Sean Manning, & Heather Sneed, thanks incalculable. Thanks to Joyce Freeland, who got me my first taxi job, and to Joey Lauren Adams, who got me my second. Thanks to Hayden Durkee for too many things to count. Thanks to Forrest Cochran for employing me behind the bar for over a decade, and to Mark Solomon for paying me to stand by highways wearing night-vision goggles (also thanks to Robert, Kim, Sox, and Shannon). Indescribable thanks to Lisa & Richard Howorth. Thanks to everyone at Tin House, especially Elizabeth DeMeo, Nanci McCloskey, Craig Popelars, Diane Chonette, Molly Templeton, & Allison Dubinsky. Thanks to my fellow UFO chasers Randy Yates, Tyler Keith, & Jeff Stockwell. Heartfelt thanks to Tom Franklin, Cody Morrison, Bill Cusumano, Pat O'Connor, Sally Frederic, Young Smith, Tim Quirk, Jim Warren, Larry Wells, Ace Atkins, Wright Thompson, Sandra Beasley, William Boyle, Jack Pendarvis, & Theresa Starkey. Special thanks to Beth & Jean Paul Mills (plus Max & Calliope!). To the Japan-US Friendship Commission, Tokyo House, the National Endowment for the Arts, the Whiting Foundation, the Trilateral Commission, and the Lakeside Toxin Football Club. Peace to the poet Hayden Carruth, who told me to get my degree and then stay the hell away from universities till I turned fifty. Peace to my mom Jean Backstrom Durkee and to my dad Peter Easton Durkee. Peace to Dean Faulkner Wells. And peace to William Buck, dead too young, for his adaptation of the *Mahabharata* after which hearing all other stories, including this one, will sound like the braying of an ass.

**NOTES**: The chapter "Hospital Runs" appeared, in a very different form, in *The Sun* magazine and now includes a quote from Dryden's *Aeneid*. The novel also uses quotes from *A Childhood: The Biography of a Place* (Harper & Row) by Harry Crews, and David Banner's "Mississippi" from the album of that name. The Bill Hicks quotes come from *Love All the People* (Soft Skull Press) by John Lahr and Bill Hicks. Lou's philosophizing is indebted to Gil Fronsdal, who wrote *The Buddha before Buddhism* (Shambhala) and to Walpola Rahula, who wrote *What the Buddha Taught* (Grove Press).

**LEE DURKEE** is the author of the novel *Rides of the Midway*. His stories and essays have appeared in *Harper's Magazine*, *The Sun*, *Best of the Oxford American*, *Zoetrope: All-Story*, *Tin House*, *New England Review*, and *Mississippi Noir*. In 2021, his memoir *Stalking Shakespeare* will chronicle his decade-long obsession with trying to find lost portraits of William Shakespeare. A former cab driver, he lives in north Mississippi.